Aiden Rolston has loved Garrett Morrison from the moment he met the vampire. Unfortunately, Fate didn't make him Garrett's beloved—his soul mate. He knows that eventually, he'll lose him—either to old age or to someone of Fate's choosing. Aiden certainly didn't think it would be to murder—his own.

Garrett's coven master always warned them not to get too attached to donors. That doesn't stop him from losing his heart to sweet Aiden, and he's the only human he's fed from in almost three years. Garrett knows the man isn't his beloved, but he just can't bring himself to look at or to touch another. Then . . . he fails him.

The Horseman of Pestilence finds the bonds his brothers—War and Death—created with their chosen ones fascinating. Their men make his brothers happy and give them companionship. Pestilence finds himself longing for the same thing, so he tells Death. When Death returns with an opportunity to create a bond with a dying human and a guilt-riddled vampire, he doesn't have long to make a choice. Can Pestilence convince the broken pair to give a bond between them a chance?

Reader Advisory: This is a M/M/M ménage.

The Hand of Pestilence
Copyright © 2020 Charlie Richards
ISBN: 978-1-4874-2986-7
Cover art by Angela Waters

Published by eXtasy Books Inc or
Devine Destinies, an imprint of eXtasy Books Inc

Look for us online at:
www.eXtasybooks.com or www.devinedestinies.com

THE HAND OF PESTILENCE
A LOVING NIP: BOOK TWENTY-TWO

BY

CHARLIE RICHARDS

DEDICATION

The difference between your mind and your heart: Your mind tells you what is smart and your heart tells you what you're going to do anyway.
~Unknown

CHAPTER ONE

"You back with me, sweetheart?"

Humming in acknowledgment of the question, Aiden Rolston pried open his eyelids. He turned his head and smiled over his shoulder at Garrett Morrison. His body pinged deliciously with aftershocks.

Gods, I love this vampire.

Just as quickly, Aiden forced himself to remember another key fact.

I'm not his beloved.

But I'll damn sure enjoy him for as long as I can.

Garrett's answering smile was full of love that caused an answering flutter in Aiden's chest.

"I'm here," Aiden whispered, not wanting to break the moment.

Rubbing his palm down Aiden's torso with his right hand, Garrett nuzzled his neck with soft lips. "Good. Love seeing you blissed-out with pleasure." His left arm was trapped under Aiden's body, and the vampire used it to clutch him to his torso. "Your body feels so perfect against mine."

Aiden hummed as he flexed his chute muscles. "And the fact that you like to keep your semi-hard dick in me for several minutes has nothing to do with it?"

"You love it, too," Garrett countered with a roll of his hips, making his still swollen length massage Aiden's inner walls. After a nip to Aiden's shoulder and another slow rut, Garrett rumbled, "Admit it."

"Oh, gods, I do," Aiden replied huskily. When Garrett

rubbed his hand over his plump belly and down to his groin to tease his shaved flesh, he groaned. "St-Stop," he whined, shivering in his lover's hold. "I-I have to work."

As a donor in the Rutherford coven located on the outskirts of Philadelphia, Aiden worked part-time on the coven grounds, same as all the others. He pulled his weight in exchange for food, lodging, a decent wage, and the privilege of offering his blood to any vampire he wished. Of course, for almost the last three years, Aiden had only shared himself with Garrett.

"I know, sweetheart," Garrett replied, stilling his movements. "I didn't mean to tease."

When Garrett cupped his jaw and urged him to turn his head, Aiden did so. He accepted a slow, thorough kiss while feeling the vampire ease his dick out of his ass. When Garrett broke away, he rolled Aiden to his back and leaned over him while threading his fingers through Aiden's hair.

"Have dinner with me this evening after you're done," Garrett murmured, his voice soft and intimate. "I have the evening shift at the guardhouse tonight. I start at eight, but I want to see you again first." His brown eyes sparkled with renewed hunger as he stared at him. "Carino's at five?"

Aiden nodded eagerly. "Yeah."

After pecking another kiss to Aiden's lips, Garrett grinned. "Good." He slid off the bed. "Come on." Holding out his hand, Garrett gave Aiden's reclining form an appreciative once-over. "If you don't get out of my bed right now" — he wiggled his fingers — "you're going to be late."

As much as Aiden would love another round on Garrett's thick rod, he knew he didn't have time. He groaned as he took the vampire's hand and pushed from the bed. Once on his own feet, Aiden released Garrett and took a step backward, lifting his hands to warn the bigger man away.

"No, I'll clean myself up," Aiden declared when Garrett

took a step toward him. "If you help, I'll still be late."

Garrett rested his hands on his hips and growled softly. "Fine. I know you're right."

For a few seconds, Aiden couldn't help but stop and stare. Naked, his feet braced apart and his hands on his hips, Garrett was a thing of masculine perfection. His lean and toned runner's build sported plenty of muscle definition in all the right places. Not one scar marred his sun-bronzed skin. Aiden loved burying his fingers in Garrett's dark brown hair, which fell to his shoulder blades in thick waves. It framed his aristocratic features to perfection.

Then Aiden's gaze slipped to Garrett's dick. Even half-soft, the appendage sported plenty of length and girth. Aiden knew from nearly three years of experience that once hard, his erection reached just over nine inches and stretched him almost to the point of pain.

But, gods, it's so worth it.

Plus, Garrett was a kind and considerate lover. He always made certain Aiden's body was ready — even when they were pressed for time and had to settle for a quickie. His vampire always sent him away with his body buzzing from pleasure.

Not my vampire.

At the thought, as always, a pang of regret surged through him.

"Aiden?"

Blinking upon hearing his name, Aiden snapped his attention back to Garrett's face. He spotted the worry in the vampire's expression and forced a bright smile. "Sorry. You fried my brain." Aiden took a step backward. "See you at Carino's."

"No," Garrett countered, shaking his head. "I'll be at your room at four-forty-five, and I'll drive us to Carino's."

"Oh!" Aiden couldn't help the surprise he felt at Garrett's pronouncement. "O-Okay."

Garrett nodded, then winked. "Now get out of here."

Aiden grinned for real that time as he grabbed his clothes and yanked them on. It sounded an awful lot like a date.

While Aiden had shared his body and blood only with Garrett for almost three years, they didn't discuss what they were doing. Almost four years ago, he'd transferred to the Rutherford coven after a vampire in his old coven had gotten too rough with him. As restitution, Aiden had asked the vampire master to find him a new home.

For the first year, Aiden had been with a number of different vampires, Garrett included. That had slowly changed. While some of the other donors thought he was a fool for getting attached to a vampire that wasn't his beloved, Aiden couldn't change what was in his heart.

Aiden passed a few people in the halls. Second Dale smiled and winked at him. He'd been with the vampire a few times that first year, but the second didn't bother approaching him anymore.

Besides, the man had several favorites he bedded regularly.

When Aiden passed fellow donor Colby, the man glared at him. He knew it was because the other guy missed being fucked by Garrett's massive cock. Colby was a size queen, and according to rumors, while Garrett didn't have the biggest dick in the coven, he was close.

Being an amazing lover probably had something to do with it, too.

Aiden ignored Colby.

After reaching his suite of rooms, Aiden took a fast shower. He brushed his wet hair, letting it fall wherever. He would need another shower after his four-hour shift in the kitchens, anyway.

No way do I want to go out to eat smelling of fry grease.

Donors rotated through different menial positions in the estate, from helping the chef to laundry to cleaning. The schedule changed monthly, designed by Enforcer Maude.

So far, Aiden had never seen her show favoritism to anyone, even donors she used herself. In the eyes of the ice queen, all donors were equal — food and labor. Aiden appreciated the fact that he was gay and had never had to service her.

Aiden pushed thoughts of everything from his mind and headed to the kitchens.

Opening the door at four-forty-five, Aiden grinned up at Garrett. His mouth watered as he took in the vampire's six-foot-two frame encased in form-fitting black jeans and a navy green button-down. The glimmer of desire in Garrett's eyes created a rush of need through Aiden.

"Hi, Aiden," Garrett greeted with a wide grin that showed off his fangs. "You look absolutely edible."

Then Garrett stepped forward, wrapped his arms around him, and pulled him flush to his bigger body.

Aiden didn't see it, but he appreciated that Garrett did. "Th-Thank you." He couldn't help how breathless he sounded. Garrett had always done that to him.

"Love how you respond to me," Garrett rumbled before sealing his mouth over Aiden's.

Aiden opened eagerly, greeting Garrett's tongue with his own. He tasted of mint, telling him the vampire had recently brushed his teeth. Under that was Garrett's natural masculine flavor that Aiden could never seem to get enough of.

Just as Aiden thought about trying to drag Garrett in for a quickie before dinner, his lover drew the kiss to an end. He loosened his arms and grabbed Aiden's fingers. With a grin on his face, Garrett swept his gaze over him again.

While Aiden was wearing his nicest jeans and a polo shirt, he knew he didn't hold a candle to Garrett.

"Come on, gorgeous." Garrett tugged him from the suite, allowing him to close the door behind him. "If I don't get you out of here now, I'm going to talk you into skipping dinner."

Aiden laughed. "I'd be amenable."

Growling, Garrett rumbled, "You're such a minx." He bent and pecked a quick kiss to Aiden's lips before continuing them forward. "One of many things I love about you."

Gasping, Aiden stumbled to a stop.

Garrett paused and helped steady him. "Aiden? You okay?"

"Y-You love me?" Aiden's heart thundered in his chest.

Sighing, Garrett nodded. "I hadn't intended to tell you like this, but you scramble my brain but good at times." He placed their threaded fingers on his chest and smiled down at Aiden. "Yeah, sweetheart. I love you." His expression turned troubled. "I know you're not my beloved, but I'm not looking for that person, either. You realize that. Right?"

Aiden hesitated.

That must have been answer enough, for Garrett sighed again. After pressing another kiss to Aiden's lips, he once more started them forward. "Let's talk over dinner," he stated. "That's when I'd intended to discuss my feelings anyway."

Nodding, Aiden walked beside Garrett in silence. Once they made it to the vampire's SUV, he blurted out, "You might not be looking, but you never know when Fate will bring that person along." Aiden reached over and gripped Garrett's wrist. "I know what happens, Garrett. The taste of my blood will begin to sour. You'll crave that other person."

Garrett growled under his breath.

Squeezing Garrett's wrist a little, Aiden admitted, "I love you, too, Garrett." When the vampire whipped his head around and stared at him with shock in his eyes, he shrugged. "I'll take you for however long Fate will let me have you. And when the time comes, yes, I'll be broken-hearted, but I always went into this with my eyes wide open, Garrett."

Resting his free hand over where Aiden gripped his wrist,

Garrett whispered hoarsely, "I don't know why Fate didn't choose you to be my beloved, Aiden."

Shrugging, Aiden had no response to that.

With a sigh, Garrett released him and started the vehicle. As he drove, he commented, "So, we're in agreement. Fate's an idiot, we love each other, and we're going to stay together for as long as we can."

Aiden chuckled, although he couldn't keep some of his sadness out of the sound.

"Move in with me," Garrett demanded. "Into my suite."

"Wh-What?" Aiden squeaked.

Garrett shrugged. "It's unorthodox, sure, but I want to know you're sleeping in my bed when I have an overnight shift."

His mind reeling, Aiden scrambled for a way to respond. *Wait.*

"Um, will Master Condor even allow that?"

"If he doesn't, we'll transfer to a coven that will."

Gaping, Aiden couldn't believe what he'd just heard. "Really?"

Garrett glanced at him before refocusing on the road. "As a heart attack."

"O-Okay." Aiden's heart swelled with excitement.

Reaching over, Garrett took Aiden's hand in his own and squeezed, a smile on his face.

Fate, please be kind and give me another couple of decades before you give Garrett his beloved.

Aiden knew it was a selfish thought, but he couldn't help himself.

After reaching the restaurant, while Aiden slid from the SUV's seat, his bladder twinged. He took Garrett's hand and grinned happily when the vampire opened the door for him. To his surprise, Garrett had made a reservation, and the hostess led them to a romantic location in the back.

When Garrett held Aiden's chair for him, he smiled and

held up his hand. "I need a minute in the men's room. Be right back."

Garrett's dark eyes smoldered as he smiled back at him. "Need help?"

Laughing, Aiden shook his head. If Garrett joined him in the bathroom, he knew exactly what would happen.

"Maybe next time."

Smirking, Garrett winked. "I'll order us a bottle of wine to celebrate."

After nodding, Aiden hurried down the hall. He stepped inside the space and hustled to a urinal. Relieving himself with a sigh, he barely acknowledged the door opening to allow another into the room.

"Don't bother doing those up," a gruff voice stated.

Whipping his head around, Aiden gaped at the stranger. His blood ran cold when he saw the way the blond man licked one of his pointed canines. He shivered as he watched the guy's irises bleed red.

Frozen to the spot, Aiden couldn't move as the strange vampire stalked toward him.

"If you can service that other vampire, you can damn well service me, donor." Then he reached for his fly.

Finally finding his voice, Aiden screamed Garrett's name, but the vampire was already on him.

CHAPTER TWO

"Master Pestilence."

Upon hearing his name called, Pestilence looked up from the scrolls he was studying. He'd received them from the Moirai that morning, and he'd been working out which demon to send where. Even with the study door closed, he'd still heard his minion.

The call was followed by a soft tapping on the wood.

"Enter," Pestilence ordered, knowing who he would see on the other side. When the door opened, he greeted the male. "Kyros, what can I do for you?"

Kyros was an old demon, coming up on his thousand-year mark. Pestilence figured he would be getting information from the Moirai about the demon's *amina* soon. He looked forward to the added prestige another bonded demon would bring him.

Pestilence and his brothers—the other Four Horsemen of the Apocalypse, War, Death, and Famine—might be getting along better these days, but he was still vain that way.

After offering a slight bow, Kyros met his gaze and stated, "Master Death is here. Are you available to see him?"

Arching one brow, Pestilence found surprise slithering through him. It wasn't a sensation he felt often. He dipped his head in a single nod.

"Show him in."

Kyros turned and exited the room.

Rising, Pestilence headed toward the other side of the massive study. He crossed to a large sideboard and opened a glass door. Pulling a decanter from inside, as well as two tumblers, he moved toward the comfortable leather chairs and sofas.

As Pestilence placed those items onto the low table set up in the middle, Death swept into the room. While everyone called them brothers, no one would say they looked it. Hell, War didn't even look humanoid unless he wanted to.

Still, of his brothers, Pestilence looked the most similar to Death. They both sported long, white-blond hair and slender frames. While Death had a tall, toned body, Pestilence appeared more gaunt, and even when he tried to straighten, he always remained a little hunched.

Death's red-irised eyes peered at him before flicking a gaze to the liquor and back again.

Pestilence knew his own eyes were an unusual pale amber.

Smiling thinly, Death pointed at the beverage. "As much as I would love to have a drink with you, brother, I'm not certain there's time."

His curiosity piqued, Pestilence cocked his head. "What happened? Something more with the angel?"

Recently, Pestilence and the others had joined forces when one of Death's demons had disappeared. His brother hadn't been able to find him, which should have been impossible. Each horseman was linked mentally to each of their demons. While they couldn't communicate telepathically or anything, they always knew where each one was and if they were healthy.

Hell, a horseman even knew when one of his demons was fucking in the human realm. None of them cared what they did after finishing an assignment. Personally, Pestilence shut the link down for a short time, and he assumed his brothers did as well.

After locating and rescuing not only Death's demon but a number of shifters and an angel — which should also *not* have been possible — the brothers had learned the extent of unrest between the humans and paranormals on that plane. They figured a war was coming. If that was the case, Pestilence had expected a call from War, not Death.

"This is not regarding the angel," Death assured, resting his scythe on the ground and gripping the shaft with both of his pale, slender hands. "Do you remember how you mentioned an interest in companionship?"

Pestilence arched a brow as surprise filled him. "I do."

Recently, after several millennia of existence alone, both War and Death had chosen to take on companions. War had bonded with a vampire and a shifter who'd been a fated match unable to complete their bond when tragedy struck. Death had chosen a pair of human lovers already in a relationship when a grievous injury threatened to separate them. His brothers split their time between the demon realm and the human one, tending to their chosen companions' needs.

Having been alone just as long as his brothers, Pestilence had found the connection fascinating, and he'd ended up longing for something similar. He'd shared that information with Death, since his job was so much more hands-on with those in the human realm. Death had promised to keep an eye out for a possible match.

Excitement flooded Pestilence.

"I've discovered a pair that may interest you," Death told him, his expression serious. "A vampire and a human."

Drawing closer to Death, Pestilence lifted his quiver from the nearby rack and slung it over his head. Next, he picked up his hunter's bow and draped it over his shoulder. Then he paused beside Death.

"I'm assuming one is near your doorstep, and that's why time is crucial," Pestilence stated. When Death nodded, he indicated that his brother should precede him from the room. "Please tell me as we walk. I'm still interested in finding companionship. If one is going to die, the other will follow, right?"

It made sense to him. A vampire couldn't live without his beloved and if bonded, vice versa for the human.

Even as Death turned and headed toward the office door, he shook his head. "They are not bonded."

"Not bonded?" Pestilence almost missed a step. "Did someone interfere, like with War's pair?"

Death again shook his head. "From the thoughts I'm getting from the vampire, they're in love and have been in a relationship for almost three years, but Fate didn't pair them."

Pestilence hummed as he strode briskly through his estate with Death at his side. "And the human?"

"He was attacked by a rogue vampire. Garrett stopped him from killing Aiden, but he did considerable damage," Death explained. "Aiden will not survive it."

"Is Garrett's beloved close at hand to ease the pain of his lover's passing?" Pestilence asked curiously.

If Fate was removing his lover, perhaps it was on purpose.

Death fell silent, and his eyes narrowed. Due to his job of removing souls from the human realm, his brother had the ability to know who was fated with whom. Of course, he was also forbidden from interfering in regards to when they found each other or even to share the knowledge.

When they reached the stable and Pestilence retrieved his mount — Death swinging onto the back of his own waiting horse — his brother finally replied.

"The shifter that Garrett is fated to is not on the east coast," Death replied thoughtfully. Meeting Pestilence's gaze with a concerned expression. "From the vampire's mental state, riddled with guilt, I fear he will lose himself in grief before they ever have a chance to meet."

Pestilence urged his horse into a gallop, seeing Death at his side, and called, "Which is why you came to me."

Death grinned, his red eyes twinkling. "Well, you *did* say you were interested in companionship."

"Indeed. I will meet them."

At that time, Pestilence and his brother reached the mists that were the gateway between realms. He reined his horse back a little, so he was a stride behind Death's animal. His senses showed him the lei line his brother targeted, and he followed him.

Pestilence appeared in the parking lot of a hospital. His natural homing instincts told him he was near Philadelphia. The warm summer afternoon wrapped around him, and he appreciated that he didn't wear a cloak like his brother. Instead, Pestilence's garments consisted of riding breeches, knee-high boots, and a comfortable tunic.

With a wave of Death's hand, his horse disappeared, and he suddenly sat on a *Harley*. His scythe became a cane, and his eyes turned green. He swung off his motorcycle and straightened the calf-length jacket he now wore.

With a wave of his own hand, Pestilence adjusted his appearance to something more suitable to the human realm. He swung off his *Harley* and followed his brother toward the hospital. Idly, he swung his own cane.

Death didn't bother stopping at the information desk, guiding him down a hall to the elevators. They reached the third floor a few seconds later. Finally, he led the way into the room.

The bowed head of the man sitting beside the bed snapped up. His brown eyes were bloodshot, and his face was damp. Even his thick brown hair stood in disarray, attesting to the fact that he must have run his fingers through it repeatedly.

This is the vampire. Garrett Morrison. Hmm . . . he's handsome despite the grief in his eyes.

"Who are you?" Garrett snapped.

"I'm someone who can help you, Garrett," Pestilence claimed, moving toward him slowly. He glanced at the human lying still on the bed. "And Aiden, too."

Garrett's nostrils flared, making it obvious he was scenting him. His eyebrows furrowed, and his body tensed. Even his grip on Aiden appeared to tighten a little.

"How—"

Before Garrett could finish his sentence, a couple of nurses bustled into the room. They immediately scowled at the horsemen. The shorter of the two hustled past them while the taller one pointed between them.

"We were told Aiden doesn't have any other family, so you should leave," she demanded.

Pestilence smiled coldly at the nurse. "We're here to support Garrett in this trying time." Pushing into her mind, he mentally urged her to go about her duties while ignoring them. "You should continue now."

Her face blanked just a little, and she did as she was told. While the shorter nurse's eyebrows furrowed, the woman didn't question the obviously superior female. They prepared to wheel Aiden from the room.

"I'll be right here waiting when you get out of surgery," Garrett whispered into Aiden's ear. Then he kissed his lover's cheek before letting go of his hand.

Once Aiden had been removed, Garrett stood and faced them, a frown curving his drawn features.

Pestilence closed the door behind them.

"I am the Horseman of Death," his brother stated. For a brief second, he revealed his true form, causing Garrett to gasp. "I think you know why I'm here."

"N-No," Garrett gasped, his eyes beginning to take on a fresh sheen. He glanced toward the closed door. "Aiden has to make it. H-He just has to." Wrapping his arms around himself, Garrett whispered, "I can't live without him."

Returning to his true form, Pestilence rested one hand on Garrett's shoulder while cradling his jaw with the other. "I said I could help. If you're willing." He hesitated a second, then added, "And if you believe Aiden would agree as well."

Garrett met Pestilence's gaze. The way the vampire's eyes moved told him he was sweeping his face. His lips tightened as his brows furrowed.

"How can you ask him?" Garrett asked. "He's unconscious, in surgery, and" — for a second, he attention flitted to Death — "not meant to survive." His voice broke as he spoke those words. "How can you help?"

"I can enter Aiden's mind, even while unconscious," Pestilence told Garrett, using his thumb to gently massage his jaw. "If he says yes to bonding with me, I'll feed him my blood, which will strengthen him enough to survive the surgery." Grimacing, he added, "While I could just pull him from the hospital, it would require altering many minds and a lot of paperwork." Pestilence shrugged. "Simpler this way."

Garrett nodded. "Anything to save Aiden."

Pestilence felt a wash of pleasure as the low burn of arousal began to simmer through him. Allowing his claws to morph from his fingernails, he lifted the forefinger of his right hand to his left wrist. He dug in deeply, slicing himself and drawing blood, then held it up for Garrett.

Upon seeing Garrett's confused expression, Pestilence arched one brow in question. "You did agree."

Then Garrett's eyes widened. "Y-You want to bond with me, too?"

"I do," Pestilence confirmed, realizing he hadn't done a very good job of explaining . . . well, *anything*. "You will *both* be my lovers, bound to me for as long as we continue to share blood." He growled softly as he added, "Fair warning. You will crave it, crave *me*, submitting to me in all ways." Reaching for Garrett's nape, Pestilence cradled it, using his hold to draw his face closer to his bleeding wrist. "Just as *I* will enjoy your companionship and giving *you* pleasure."

"But I failed Aiden," Garrett whispered, even as his nostrils flared and his focus riveted on Pestilence's blood. His desire was clear in his eyes as they bled to red. "Why would you want someone who couldn't protect his lover?"

"That was not your fault," Pestilence stated simply.

"Better hurry," Death cut in. "Aiden doesn't have much time."

Pestilence nodded just a little, indicating that he'd heard. "Well?" His heart pounded in anticipation.

Finally, Garrett nodded. Then he leaned forward and grabbed hold of Pestilence's wrist. After just a second more of hesitation, Garrett wrapped his lips around Pestilence's bleeding flesh. He swiped his tongue to catch the blood before groaning and sinking his fangs into him.

Feeling the exquisite sensation of Garrett drinking from him, Pestilence moaned. His cock throbbed in his breeches, and his knees threatened to buckle. He trembled as his balls tightened.

Before Pestilence could harness control, his testicles pulled up, and with a growl and a buck of his hips, he came. Shuddering, he unloaded behind his fly. Spots danced across his vision as trembles worked through him.

"Hurry," Death whispered into his ear.

Pestilence gasped as he came back to himself. He realized Garrett had stopped drinking, and the wound was sealed. Shaking his head, he took in the vampire's flushed face.

The smell of cum perfumed the air, and it wasn't all his own.

"Damn," Pestilence whispered. "Forgot about that little perk of vampires."

Garrett shifted on his feet, appearing uncomfortable.

Chuckling softly, Pestilence murmured, "Next time, I'll use my tongue, but since we don't have time now . . ." With a wink and a wave of his hand, Pestilence used magick to clean up both their releases. "There. Now I'll speak with Aiden, and as soon as we can, we'll return to my realm to complete our bonds."

After getting a small nod from Garrett, Pestilence strode from the room. Death remained behind.

Pestilence jogged through the corridors, swiftly finding the room he wanted. Cloaking himself in invisibility, he entered. Frowning upon spotting the tube down Aiden's throat, Pestilence dug into the minds of the doctor and nurses working on the human, giving them the image that the tube remained even as he gently removed it. Next, he sprouted his wings from his back, tearing through his tunic. Wrapping them around Aiden's head, Pestilence whispered an ancient spell, connecting his mind to the human's.

Pestilence whispered into Aiden's mind.

Sweet Aiden, do you wish to live? To stay with Garrett?

Yes. The man's response was immediate.

Pestilence smiled.

What if it meant you had to share him and yourself with another lover?

After a second of hesitation, Aiden spoke again. *With his beloved?*

No. Pestilence heard beeping and the doctor shouting orders. *We don't have much time, sweet Aiden. If you accept my blood, you will be bound to me and Garrett for all time. We will be yours, and you will be ours.*

Who are you?

I am the Horseman of Pestilence. His heart skipped a beat in his chest as he spotted the resuscitation paddles. *Does it matter? You're about to die.*

Anything to stay with Garrett.

Satisfaction flooded Pestilence, and he swiftly sliced his wrist for the second time that day. He placed it at Aiden's lips. *Drink.*

Aiden did, and Pestilence poured healing energy into his human's chest, allowing the paddles to do their job and his heart to beat once more.

17

CHAPTER THREE

Garrett paced the room, unease churning in his gut. Swallowing hard, he could still taste the flavor of Pestilence's blood on his tongue. He flushed as he remembered his response to the horseman.

Gods, I came in my pants from his delicious flavor.

While Garrett had caused many people to do the same over the course of his nearly two centuries of life, he hadn't done that himself since he was an adolescent.

Rubbing the back of his neck, Garrett felt guilt claw at him. He didn't deserve Aiden's forgiveness, no matter how much he desired it. His human had been gravely injured. Glancing Death's way as he made another pass of the room, he acknowledged that he would have, *should* have died.

A small smile suddenly curved Death's lips. He didn't push off the wall on which he leaned, his right ankle crossed over his left. Death did turn his head and focus on him, however.

"Aiden accepted Pestilence's offer," Death told him, appearing pleased. "He lives."

"He wasn't supposed to, was he?" Garrett forced his feet to stop moving, and he crossed his arms over his chest. "He was supposed to die . . . because I didn't get to him in time." As he watched Death's eyes narrow, he continued. "I should have—"

"You have no control over when someone is supposed to die," Death stated, interrupting Garrett's rambling. "When it is time, it is time."

"Then why—" Before Garrett could finish his question about why Pestilence would step in, the door of the room banged open, and three vampires strode inside. Garrett dipped his head in deference. "Enforcer Caine."

Garrett knew the other two were Enforcer Rizer and Enforcer Whitney, but Caine was the head enforcer, so he addressed him.

"You were ordered back to the coven after we cleaned up the mess at the restaurant," Enforcer Caine pointed out, a disapproving look on his face.

Swallowing hard, Garrett felt his face flush. "I—" He paused, cleared his throat, then tried again. "I didn't want Aiden to wake up and be alone."

Caine heaved a deep sigh as he shook his head. "I know you're especially attached to the donor, but his chances of survival are extremely slim." The dark-haired vampire frowned at him. "You should've followed orders. Now Master Condor has requested your presence." Then Caine tapped his watch. "It didn't help that you skipped out on your guard shift without notice or getting a replacement."

Garrett grimaced. He'd completely forgotten about his shift. All he'd been able to think about was his sweet Aiden lying so still in a hospital bed. He'd poured his anguish into his silent prayers to the gods.

And Pestilence came.

That caused Garrett to remember Death's presence. Except, when he looked around, the horseman was gone.

"Are you coming in quietly, Garrett?" Enforcer Caine asked, his tone deep with concern.

A soft voice Garrett recognized as Death's whispered into his ear, nearly making him jump out of his skin. He barely contained his shock upon hearing the horseman's offer.

"You are no longer bound to that coven, Garrett," Death told him. "Say the word, and I'll send them on their way."

Shaking his head just a smidge, Garrett muttered, "I don't

want to cause trouble, and I need to let Master Condor know I'm leaving."

"As you wish," Death replied. "I'll let Pestilence know where you went."

"I know I have no right to ask it of you," Garrett began, unable to help himself. "But will you make certain Aiden doesn't wake up alone?"

"Who are you talking to?" Enforcer Rizer snapped, scowling.

Death chuckled. "Only you can hear me. Make up whatever story you wish." He squeezed Garrett's upper arm, perhaps in sympathy. "Your Aiden will be well taken care of from now on."

Garrett nodded once, then stepped forward. "I'll go quietly." Upon spotting Rizer's suspicious look, he added, "And I was discussing options with the invisible devil on my shoulder, but the angel on the other one won out."

Even as Rizer sneered, clearly not believing him—although what he said was true from a certain point of view, and Garrett's scent didn't give off the odor of deceit—Death laughed from behind him.

"Good thing," Enforcer Caine stated with a snort. He rested his hand on Garrett's upper arm. "Let's get this over with."

As Garrett headed out of the room, he didn't fight Caine's hold. Reaching the hall, the head enforcer released him and fell into step to his right. Rizer and Whitney followed behind them.

Upon reaching the parking lot, Garrett pulled out his keys. When Whitney held up her palm, he handed them to her. He pointed, indicating the direction where he'd parked, since Caine was leading him another way.

Garrett felt unease churn through his gut for a new reason

when Enforcer Rizer slid into the back seat beside him. Peering out the window, he wondered what he'd done to create such animosity in the vampire. While he and Rizer had never been friendly, he found the enforcer's blatant distaste for him a little odd.

"Enforcer Caine," Garrett began slowly, trying to sort his thoughts. "Did Master Condor say why he ordered me back to the estate as opposed to going to the hospital?"

When Garrett had first heard the order, he'd thought it was for no other reason than Master Condor wanted his report first hand. He'd dismissed it and gone to the hospital, instead. Garrett had figured he could just beg forgiveness later, once he'd been assured that Aiden would be okay.

Unfortunately, that hadn't been the case, and the staff had immediately begun prepping Aiden for surgery. He'd used his vampiric trancing ability to allow him to stay in the same room as his lover. If he'd been human, he knew he would have been sent to a waiting room.

"I'm sorry, Garrett," Caine replied. "I don't know."

"Second Dale spotted Garrett returning to his room." Rizer's voice held a definite sneer to his tone. "Still using the same donor, Garrett?" He curled his lip. "Such a disgrace, falling for a damn donor. Especially *that* one."

Garrett barely repressed his growl. The vampire was an enforcer for the coven, after all. He was much higher on the totem pole than him.

"Who I choose to feed from is no one's business but my own," Garrett stated, frowning out the window. "And what do you mean by especially *that one?*"

"He's fat and plain," Rizer snapped with a scoff. "No wonder Fate didn't make Aiden your beloved. He's not worthy of bonding with a vampire."

That time, Garrett wasn't able to bite back his snarl. Snapping his attention to Rizer, he glared at the other vampire.

"Aiden is sweet and kind and funny. His body is perfect, and I would have been *honored* if Fate had gifted me with him as my beloved."

While Fate hadn't granted him the human, Garrett realized that Pestilence had given him the greatest gift possible.

I'll be bound to him always.

Garrett found himself grinning.

"What are *you* so happy about?" Rizer snapped. His eyes narrowed. "I think you talkin' back is a punishable offense. I'm gonna tell Master Condor that—"

"Rizer," Enforcer Caine barked. "That's enough."

"But, Caine," Rizer began, his expression turning petulant. "He countered me. I'm an enforcer, and he's just a guard. He—"

Enforcer Caine frowned over his shoulder at Rizer, causing the other enforcer to shut his trap. "We just forced Garrett to leave his lover in the hospital while having surgery," he pointed out. "His emotions were high, to begin with. Besides, all he was doing was defending his injured lover."

Garrett sighed deeply, calming down. At least the head enforcer understood. To his relief, everyone fell silent after that. Although, to Garrett, Rizer appeared to be pouting.

Why did Master Condor make this asshole an enforcer?

Then another thought struck him.

Now I won't have to deal with him anymore.

To Garrett's surprise, he didn't feel a bit of sadness at the fact that he would have to leave the Rutherford coven. He'd been there for nearly forty years, so it was high time he thought about moving on anyway. Of course, it had been easy to ignore the need since he'd rarely had to leave the place because he had Aiden as a regular donor. Garrett hadn't needed to go into town to get blood from a stranger when he hadn't been interested in other donors, as he had prior to Aiden's arrival.

Caine driving through the front gate of their coven's estate pulled Garrett out of his thoughts. He spotted Enforcer Maude waiting on the front steps, and a fresh wave of uncertainty flooded him. The fact that Master Condor intended to have three enforcers attend him was . . . concerning.

"Wow," Enforcer Caine muttered, obviously noting the significance, too. He glanced in the mirror as he parked and met Garrett's gaze before shrugging his shoulders.

Fighting back a sigh, Garrett opened his door and slipped out. He closed his door at the same time Caine did, and they headed around the hood together. With his hands shoved into his jacket's pockets, he tried to keep himself relaxed.

Enforcer Maude beckoned, her expression blandly cool. The woman always seemed to appear bored, as if whatever duty she was performing was beneath her. At least she didn't appear upset.

I've seen that once, and never want her rage directed my way.

"Enforcer Caine," Maude greeted with a slight dip of her head. She was the second enforcer, so she ignored Rizer.

"Enforcer Maude," Caine replied back. "Is Master Condor waiting?"

Maude nodded. "Yeah." She trained her focus on Garrett. "You kinda screwed up on this one," she commented mildly as she turned and headed up the stairs, leading the way. "The master was already annoyed with you. Bad time to disobey him."

Garrett couldn't help but ask, "Why was he annoyed with me?"

Scoffing, Maude side-eyed him. "Uh, you monopolized a donor. Aiden hasn't allowed any vampire but you to take his blood . . . for a couple of years now." Her tone made it sound as if Garrett was dumb for asking. "We pay for his food and keep a roof over his head. He's supposed to be a donor, but you're the only one using him."

Oh fuck.

"He was going to be let go, anyway, if he didn't start accepting others."

Maude dropped that bombshell as if it was nothing.

Biting back a groan, Garrett realized he hadn't considered how his leaders would perceive their *relationship*.

"Then you go and ignore the master's order to be with Aiden." Maude rolled her eyes. "Not smart, man."

Garrett couldn't remember ever hearing Maude offer so much information. "I love Aiden," he admitted on a whisper. "We didn't mean for that to happen. We just—"

"*Love* him?" Rizer cut in, sounding scandalized. "That fat fuck? Seriously?"

To Garrett's relief, Caine cuffed Rizer up the backside of his head. "Stop being a superficial prat," he grumbled.

Maude acted as if she hadn't heard either of their comments. She waved her hand in the air. "Anyway. Just agree with whatever the master orders, and you'll be fine."

"Yes, Enforcer," Garrett murmured, pulling one hand from his pocket to rub the back of his neck. "Thank you for explaining."

Grunting softly, Maude paused before Master Condor's closed office door. She knocked twice. After hearing the master's order for them to enter, she opened the door and led the way inside.

Master Condor stood near his window, his back to them. The broad-shouldered blond vampire had his hands clasped behind him and peered outside. For a moment, he didn't acknowledge them.

Garrett had been standing there for a good two minutes, sweat beading on his temples, before the vampire turned and pinned his blue-eyed gaze on him.

"I have warned those under my care time and time again," Master Condor began, his voice deep and firm. "Do *not* get attached to donors." His eyes narrowed as he pinned him with a disappointed look. "Should Aiden Rolston live, he will no longer be employed here. His mind will be wiped, and he will be set up in another city. You *will* leave him to his life."

"No." The whispered word was out of Garrett's mouth before he could censure himself.

Master Condor's lips pinched. "I thought that might be your response." He snapped his fingers, and Rizer grabbed his upper arms. "Take him to the cells."

His blood running cold, Garrett struggled.

Pain exploded through the back of his head, and darkness took him.

CHAPTER FOUR

"Where's Garrett?"

Pestilence swept his gaze around the room as if taking a second look would make his missing vampire appear. Just as before, only Death waited.

Death rose from the chair he'd been lounging in. "Several vampire enforcers showed up to get him. They claimed he had gone against his coven master's order by coming to the hospital," his brother explained, shaking his head and frowning. "I offered to send them on their way without him, since he no longer has to answer to them." Death grimaced, crossing his arms over his chest. "Garrett turned me down and went with them. Just asked me to make certain Aiden didn't wake up alone."

Heaving a sigh, Pestilence growled under his breath. "Very well. I'll go get him."

Nodding, Death pointed out, "When War started his bond with his chosen vampire, he was able to communicate telepathically right away. Perhaps you should try him that way? See if he's ready to leave?"

Pestilence hummed. "Even before fucking and biting him?"

"Yes," Death confirmed. "Just from him taking War's blood."

Closing his eyes, Pestilence tipped his head back. He mentally scanned his being, searching . . . and found the faint bonds that had already formed. Feeling along them, Pestilence quickly figured out which went to Aiden and which led to Garrett.

Doing his best to push into Garrett's mind, Pestilence called to him.

Garrett? Can you hear me?

After a moment without a response, Pestilence tried again.

Garrett, my chosen. Can you hear me?

Pestilence waited another minute, then opened his eyes and shook his head. "Either it hasn't formed, or I'm doing it wrong. I'm not getting a response."

"Or he's asleep," Death pointed out.

Scoffing, Pestilence shook his head. "No way is Garrett at the estate sleeping while Aiden is here coming out of surgery."

"Ah. Of course," Death said, conceding the point. "So you're going to get him."

"Yes," Pestilence confirmed. "I'm certain he'd prefer to be here, and it'll give me a chance to inform Condor that Garrett no longer answers to him."

Tugging along a different mental thread, Pestilence sent a summons to one of his demons.

"Garrett asked that someone stay here for Aiden," Death reminded him. "One of us needs to stay, and I really should return to my duties."

Pestilence chuckled as he smirked at his brother. "You mean return to Daren and Eric," he teased, referring to Death's two chosen companions. "And I won't leave Aiden unattended. I've summoned Kyros. I'm certain he'll be here directly."

Death grinned, his red eyes dancing with mirth. "Yes, I do miss my humans." Heading toward the door, he waved his good-bye as he called, "I wish you all the best with your men, Pestilence."

"Thank you, brother."

Pausing, Death peered at him over his shoulder. "Should you need assistance . . ."

His brother left the sentence unfinished, but Pestilence understood. "Again, thank you." He dipped his head in appreciation.

Then Death was gone, and Pestilence found himself alone in a hospital for the first time in . . . ever. He heaved a sigh and settled in the chair to wait. Then he thought better of it.

Knowing his demon would be able to track him within the hospital regardless of his location, Pestilence returned to Aiden's side. He remained invisible to human eyes as he strode back to where his human was having surgery performed on him. His chosen was just being sewn up after they'd repaired his ruptured spleen.

Pestilence watched the humans get to work on Aiden's broken leg next. As much as he wished he could whisk the man out of the hospital and heal him immediately, he bided his time. After Aiden was released — which would be sooner rather than later — he would take his pretty human to his home and heal everything.

Just thinking of laying Aiden out before the dancing purple flames of his bedroom's massive fireplace caused a stirring in Pestilence's loins. He reached down and cupped himself, absently rubbing his growing erection. It had been a while — maybe centuries — since he'd bothered jacking off, and now he couldn't wait to explore Aiden's body.

And Garrett's, too.

That meant Pestilence needed to collect his vampire.

Just as Pestilence began to grow impatient, Kyros jogged into the room. None of the humans reacted to his arrival, telling him his demon remained as invisible as he. The tall, pale-skinned male wore only a pair of jeans as he peered around with interest, his white wings billowing behind him.

"Master Pestilence," Kyros greeted with a dip of his head. "How may I assist you?"

"This is Aiden Rolston," Pestilence told him, pointing at the sandy-blond-haired human on the operating table. "I have chosen to bond with him and a vampire named Garrett Morrison."

"Really?" Kyros's silver-colored eyes shown with interest as he stared at Aiden. "Congratulations, Master."

"Thank you." Pestilence grinned, pleasure filling him at Kyros's instant acceptance. "Garrett was pulled away by some enforcers. I'm going to get him."

Kyros tilted his head, his attention returning to Pestilence. "Do you require me to accompany you? Do you fear there will be trouble?"

Pestilence hadn't considered the possibility of trouble. Even if there was, there was nothing a vampire could throw at him that he couldn't handle. Between his power as a Horseman of the Apocalypse and his magick, Pestilence could probably wipe out the entire coven without breaking a sweat.

Of course, Fate would probably be pissed if I did.

With that thought tripping through his mind, Pestilence felt his lips twitch with mirth. "No, Kyros. I don't want Aiden to possibly awake alone while I'm gone collecting my other chosen," he explained to his demon. "Put on a non-threatening form and remain by his side. Do whatever it takes to remain in his room."

Kyros bowed deeply. "I'm honored to assist."

As Kyros straightened, his wings eased into his back. His facial features altered, his sharp teeth disappearing and his ears losing their pointedness. The claws on his hands retracted, tan cowboy boots appeared on his feet, and a flannel shirt covered his bare chest.

"Stay invisible until Aiden is taken to a room," Pestilence instructed. "I'll be back as swiftly as possible."

"Yes, Master," Kyros replied with another dip of his head. "I'll be here."

Pestilence strode from the room, eager to collect his other chosen. After leaving the hospital, he swung aboard his motorcycle and brought it roaring to life. Steering his bike out of the lot, Pestilence smiled in anticipation of seeing his vampire again.

Even rough from grief, Garrett's handsomeness was apparent. He couldn't wait to slide his palms all over his toned, lean body. As he thought about massaging his muscled thighs and spreading them, his prick throbbed behind his fly. He'd been hard even while giving orders to his demon, and he looked forward to putting his erection to good use.

Soon.

While Pestilence could have used a lei line to pop into the Rutherford coven estate, he chose to drive instead and announce himself at the gate. If Garrett had enough loyalty to return when summoned even if he no longer needed to, he figured his vampire wanted to remain on good terms with his prior coven. Pestilence knew that War's vampire still worked with his coven, so perhaps Garrett felt the same desire.

Reaching the gate, Pestilence pressed the button on the call box.

"Who is it?" A female voice came through the speaker.

Holding down the button, Pestilence stated, "I am the Horseman of Pestilence, here to see Master Condor."

After a couple of heartbeats, the woman stuttered, "Wh-Who?"

"I am Pestilence, one of the Four Horsemen of the Apocalypse." Pestilence smirked. "Open the gate, Karlita."

"How do you — How do you know who I am?" There was a definite note of fear there.

Fighting back his urge to roll his eyes, Pestilence told her, "I am a horseman. I know the names of everyone." All his brothers did. Knowing names was required to fulfill their duties.

"Um, I have a guard headed your way to verify your identity and escort you," Karlita stated, clearly uneasy. "I'll let the master know you're here."

"Thank you, Karlita."

Straddling his bike, Pestilence waited impatiently. He spotted a blond-haired vampire appear from the left. Immediately, Pestilence's nature supplied a name.

Spade Sanchez.

"You're a Horseman of the Apocalypse?" The man grinned crookedly at him through the gate. His expression screamed his disbelief. "Where's your horse?"

Pestilence arched his left brow as he glanced around the area. Seeing no one else around, he snapped his fingers. Instantly, he no longer rode a *Harley*, his horse returning to her true form.

Spade gaped.

"Any other questions, Spade?" Pestilence asked dryly.

"Damn," Spade muttered, expressing his amazement. "Sorry, uh . . . I'm not sure how to address you." As Spade spoke, he hit a button, causing the gate to open.

"Master Pestilence is fine," Pestilence replied, urging his horse to start forward.

Spade nodded. "Of course, Master Pestilence." Then he spoke into a microphone strapped to his shoulder. "I'm en route with Master Pestilence."

"It's really him?" That was Karlita's voice.

"Uh, near as I can tell," Spade admitted.

Pestilence urged his horse into a lope, eager to see Garrett. As a vampire, Spade had no trouble keeping up. His vampire abilities gave him impressive speed.

A large estate appeared around a bend in the paved driveway. His horse's hooves clopped in measured rhythm as he approached. He swept his gaze over the place, noticing the security cameras and gorgeously manicured lawn.

Watching the front door open, Pestilence fought a smirk as three vampires exited. *Caine, Maude, and Rizer.* He knew those three were enforcers for the coven.

Pestilence figured the show of strength was meant to intimidate, but since he could wipe the floor with them, it was lost on him.

Stopping under the massive portico, Pestilence swung from his saddle. He hefted his bow higher on his shoulder before heading toward the steps. Sweeping his gaze over the trio, he took in their wary expressions.

Focusing on Caine, Pestilence stated, "Enforcer Caine. Are you to escort me to Master Condor?"

Enforcer Caine seemed startled for an instant, obviously surprised at being called by name. "Yes, sir." Glancing beyond Pestilence, he stated, "I'll take it from here, Spade."

"Yes, Enforcer Caine." Then Spade moved off, probably to return to his rounds or whatever else he was supposed to be doing.

Pestilence started forward, not waiting to be invited.

While Enforcer Caine turned to lead the way, the others waited for him to pass. Then the pair fell into step, flanking Pestilence.

Glancing around, Pestilence didn't bother noting the décor. He was searching for his chosen. It had probably been wishful thinking to see him just wandering around the hallways, but he already missed his vampire. Pestilence would use their blood bond to track him down after meeting with Condor.

Pay respects first.

After Enforcer Caine knocked on a closed door, Pestilence heard someone call, "Enter."

Enforcer Caine opened the door and led the way inside.

Pestilence spotted Master Condor seated behind a large wooden desk. Second Dale stood behind his right shoulder. The enforcers filed in around Pestilence as he stopped before the desk.

Master Condor's smile was as fake as his words as he asked, "To what do I owe the honor of your visit, Horseman of Pestilence?" Then he waved toward a chair to Pestilence's left. "Would you care to have a seat? A drink?"

"That is unnecessary," Pestilence replied, deciding to get

right down to business. "I came to greet you as is customary when entering another paranormal leader's territory." He dipped his head in a slight nod, recognizing Condor as the coven master. "After our meeting, I intend to assist Garrett in packing his and Aiden's belongings."

His eyes narrowing, Master Condor scowled at Pestilence. "Aiden is no longer part of this coven, so you're welcome to take his things to him if that is your wish," he declared. "But you have no cause to do the same to Garrett's, however. He is my guard and will continue to reside here under my leadership."

Great. Posturing.

"No, Master Condor," Pestilence stated, deciding blunt was best. "Both Aiden and Garrett are my chosen bonded ones. They are both now mine."

Master Condor rose to his feet. Resting his knuckles on his desk, he leaned forward. "You cannot just take whoever you wish," he stated, curling his lip and showing off one fang. "Garrett is *my* man, and he doesn't have permission to leave."

Pestilence scoffed. "I asked them, and they accepted. None of us need your permission." He began to turn, tossing over his shoulder, "I didn't even need to ask for permission to enter. Now I will get my chosen."

Between one step and the next, Pestilence disappeared. He pulled along a lei line, seeking the thread of Garrett's bond. Locating it, Pestilence reappeared inside a room.

Anger surged through Pestilence as he took in the space and the state of his chosen vampire.

Garrett is unconscious in a cage. Oh, fuck no!

Only Pestilence's desire to get Garrett safe and healthy kept him from returning to the study and slaughtering the vampires within that room.

Lifting Garrett into his arms, Pestilence took them first to the portico to retrieve his mount, then to the hospital.

Lying Garrett on an empty hospital bed, Pestilence used a

glamour spell to hide them from prying eyes. Then he set about healing him of his cuts and bruises.

When you wake, my vampire, you will have some explaining to do.

Chapter Five

The steady *bip, bip* noise told Aiden where he was even before he noticed the smell of antiseptic. The pain registered next, throbbing through his abdominals, down his left leg, and through his left wrist. His throat felt scratchy, and his mouth seemed to be filled with cotton balls.

Aiden searched his pain-filled mind for memories on how he'd ended up in the hospital. The images that burst across his brain caused a whimper to erupt from him. A hard shudder worked through his body, creating a fresh wash of agony along his nerve endings.

"Easy, chosen of the master," a deep voice crooned. "You are safe. You will soon be well."

Not recognizing the man's voice, when Aiden felt the touch to his right arm, he cringed.

"Hush, Aiden," the man urged again. "I will soothe you."

To Aiden's surprise, the stranger said something in a guttural language he couldn't understand. Almost instantly, the pain eased. His body no longer throbbed with each beat of his heart.

After swallowing, or trying to, Aiden licked his lips. Opening his mouth, he forced himself to whisper, "Water." Okay, it came out more like a rasp.

Still, Aiden must have gotten his point across. "These are ice chips," the stranger told him before something cold rubbed over his lower lip. "Let's start with these to get some moisture into your mouth. Then I'll summon some water for you."

Aiden accepted the chip into his mouth and sighed. The small bit of ice melting on his tongue felt fantastic. After swallowing, he opened his mouth for more.

The stranger complied.

After giving him three more ice chips, the man asked, "Are you ready for some water?"

"Yes, please," Aiden managed to murmur.

Once again, the man said something in that same unknown language. Then—"Here's a straw."

Aiden felt something poke his lips, so he opened them. Accepting the straw, he sucked lightly. Cool, clean water flowed across his tongue, tasting beyond delicious.

Once Aiden had had enough, he used his tongue to push the straw out of his mouth. He sighed. Between the weird soothing thing the stranger had done and the water to remove the scratchiness and cotton filling his mouth and throat, Aiden didn't feel too bad.

Lifting his right hand, Aiden gently rubbed at his eyes. He managed to open them as he returned his hand to the bed. Turning his head, he peered at the guy sitting beside him.

Huh.

"Who are you?"

Aiden figured that wasn't the most important question, but it was the one that came from him. With the stranger's pale, slender features and odd silver-blue eyes, he was pretty sure he would have remembered meeting him. The guy's wide smile as he tended to Aiden told him he was truly happy to be there.

"It's good to see you open your eyes, chosen of the master," the guy told him. He used his empty hand to touch his chest. "I am Kyros, one of the master's minions."

Ooooookay.

"Um, who's your master?" Aiden asked, because really, this guy saying he was the master's chosen seemed odd. He'd never heard of anyone referring to another that way, even in the paranormal world.

Kyros narrowed his eyes and tipped his head. "Why, Master Pestilence, of course."

Pestilence?

The name jogged another memory.

Aiden had been floating in darkness. Confused and aching to feel Garrett's arms around him one last time, he'd known he was dying. His soul had cried with despair, knowing it would never happen.

Then . . . a voice had whispered in his mind. He'd been offered a choice. Live and share Garrett with Pestilence, a Horseman of the Apocalypse, or die. While Aiden hadn't been certain it was really happening, he'd taken the chance at being able to stay.

"Wow," Aiden murmured, swallowing hard. "That was real." Then he glanced around the room. "Um, wh-where is he?"

Gods, please let Pestilence be a man.

"He'll be back as soon as he can," Kyros assured him. "He went to the coven to pick up Garrett." His pale brows furrowing, he glanced toward the clock on the wall. "I'm surprised he's not back already. It's been over an hour and a half."

"I ran into some trouble," a melodious-sounding tenor filled the room before the male appeared.

Thank the gods.

Aiden's lips parted as he took in the man who'd spoken. He was tall, maybe six-foot-five or six, but with the way he stooped just a smidge, it was tough to tell. His white-blond hair flowed over his shoulders, nearly reaching his waist. While his features appeared a little gaunt and there was a sallowness to his skin, his gorgeous pale-amber eyes were what truly drew Aiden's attention.

"Oh." Aiden felt his heart speed up in his chest. His fingers actually twitched with his desire to thread them through the man's long hair. He wanted to know what those silky-looking strands felt like. "Wow."

A familiar husky rumble drew Aiden's attention.

To Aiden's pleasure, Garrett accompanied Pestilence, although he looked a little rough. He still wore the same clothes as when they'd been on their date, but they were torn and bloodied. His left eye was almost swollen shut, and he limped a little on his right leg.

Still, Garrett grinned crookedly at him. "Hi, sweet Aiden."

"Garrett," Aiden whispered, glancing between the two men. "I . . . I . . . what happened?"

"Your ex-coven is run by an asshole," Pestilence declared, his tone hardening. His eyes narrowed, and a snarl rumbled from him. "You'll not be returning there."

Aiden knew the anger wasn't directed at him. He really did. However, coupled with the snarl and fierce expression as well as the pointed teeth, his pulse sky-rocketed. Aiden suddenly felt fangs at his neck and dirty tile beneath his knees.

Opening his mouth, Aiden tried to scream, to call for help, but nothing came from his too-dry throat.

"Whoa, Aiden. Easy, sweetheart. Easy."

Garrett's deep voice penetrated the fog that had descended over Aiden's mind. He whimpered and reached toward the sound. Pain stabbed through his arm, and he cringed back.

Aiden registered a touch to his temple. Then everything went dark.

A cocoon of softness cradled Aiden's body. He felt relaxed and comfortable. The heavy arm around his waist was familiar.

Except, this is not Garrett's bed.

And wasn't I injured?

Blinking open his eyes, Aiden brought the room into focus. He stared up at a light green ceiling. Hearing crackling, he turned his head.

Shock flooded his system.

"The fire is purple," Aiden mumbled, taking in the dancing flames in the huge bowl atop the pedestal. More noise pulled his attention, and he realized there were similar fire-pedestals in each corner of the room, illuminating the large space.

"They are indeed."

Hearing the soft tenor, Aiden snapped his attention to a pair of comfortable-looking chairs near a massive fireplace. The hearth was set up for a fire but hadn't been lit. In one of the chairs sat Pestilence.

"Oh." Aiden felt a smile curving his lips, and he once again felt the need to slide his fingers through the man's long pale hair. "Hi."

Real eloquent, Aiden.

"Hello, Aiden." Pestilence placed the black goblet he'd been holding on a nearby side table. "I didn't mean to frighten you earlier, my sweet chosen. Are you feeling better?"

"Frighten me?" Aiden racked his brain, trying to figure out what the other man was talking about. Recalling his panic attack, he winced. "Gods, it wasn't you. I . . . I saw your anger and —" Aiden paused, shaking his head. "I didn't mean to freak out."

Pestilence nodded slowly. His amber-eyed gaze roved over Aiden's face, as if searching for the truth of his words. He seemed to find it, for he offered a small smile.

"We should be sure to share that with Garrett when he wakes. We need to learn your triggers, so we can avoid them." Pestilence's smile twisted into something that appeared a little pained. "I should have realized an attack like that would cause mental trauma. Should we find a therapist?"

"Um." Aiden really just wanted to forget the whole thing. Still, if his brain kept fritzing out any time he heard someone get upset, that wouldn't work very well. "Can we play it by ear and see?"

"Of course, Aiden," Pestilence replied. "Whatever you wish." Then he swept his gaze over Aiden's form again before returning his attention to his face. "But you didn't answer how you felt. Any residual pain?"

Aiden peered down his body, seeing his chest bare and a blanket pulled up to his waist. From the feel of the fabric on his ass, he knew he wore nothing. That wasn't the most startling thing, however.

"I'm not wearing any casts or bandages." Aiden snapped his focus back to Pestilence. "How is that possible?"

Pestilence's body tensed and leaned forward, almost as if he were preparing to rise. Instead, he settled back into his chair. He even gripped the arms, as if he needed to physically grab something to keep himself still.

"The first few times a person passes through the veil that separates the human realm from the demon one, they pass out," Pestilence told him. "After I removed you from the hospital, I took advantage of your continued unconsciousness and healed your injuries while you rested, as well as Garrett's." His fingers twitched as he roved his gaze over Aiden's chest. "I don't think I missed anything, and I hoped there wouldn't be any residual discomfort."

Aiden's lips parted, surprise flooding him. "Wow. Thank you." He wiggled his toes and rubbed his arms with his opposite hands. "I, uh, I feel great."

In fact, between the feel of Garrett's naked body next to his own and the handsome man sitting not too far away, certain parts of Aiden were feeling very well indeed.

"I'm glad to hear it," Pestilence replied softly.

"So, um." Aiden shifted restlessly, which only caused his shaft to harden more swiftly.

Pestilence's nostrils flared, proving he could smell Aiden's arousal. The horseman's Adam's apple bobbed, and he licked his lips. His amber eyes narrowed.

"H-How does bonding with a horseman work?" Aiden blurted out the question. "Is it like, uh, bonding between a vampire and his beloved?"

Aiden's cock twitched as he wondered how Pestilence's pale skin would feel beneath his fingers.

"Yes," Pestilence replied, his voice deepening a little. "I will spill in you both, drink your blood, and you will drink from me." After clearing his throat, he added, "You will come to crave my blood, Aiden, and continue to live for as long as you continue to accept me."

His heart rate sky-rocketed as he thought about what Pestilence's lean body looked like under his breeches and tunic. He felt goose bumps break out on his skin. Gripping the comforter beneath him, he twisted it between his fingers.

While Aiden couldn't figure out why he wanted that so badly, he—

"You already fed me your blood once," Aiden murmured, latching onto the murky memory. "In the hospital."

"I did."

Aiden met Pestilence's eyes. "I think I'm already feeling some of that craving." Cocking his head, he asked, "Aren't you interested in finishing what we started?"

Just the thought that Pestilence wouldn't want to complete their bond started his pulse spiking for a new reason.

"I want to finish what we started very much," Pestilence admitted, his tone a little gruff. "It is taking every ounce of willpower I have to stay seated here." His fingers tightened on his chair's arms. "Revealing your beautiful skin while healing you, I became so hard so fast. Been so very long since I've felt such need."

Reaching down, Pestilence pressed his palm against his crotch.

Aiden gasped upon seeing the lovely outline of Pestilence's long, slender erection. His mouth watered, and his ass clenched. He couldn't see all of it, and he wanted to oh-so-badly.

"Then why are you sitting over there?" Aiden asked, panting softly.

"You panicked, and I worried you were afraid of me."

Shaking his head, Aiden whispered, "Not afraid of you."

Garrett moaned from beside him, his arm tightening around his waist. His vampire nuzzled his neck, and Aiden immediately tipped his head to offer more room. A soft growl erupted from his lover.

"Love how you smell," Garrett rumbled. "I smell your need."

"Open your eyes," Aiden ordered, still staring at Pestilence. His heart tripped in his chest as he saw the unbridled lust darkening the horseman's eyes.

"Aiden?" Garrett lifted his head and peered around. "Oh, wow."

"Mmm-hmmm." Aiden focused on Garrett and grinned. "I really wanna invite our new lover to our bed." Realizing what he said, he chuckled, "Or maybe ask him to join us in *his* bed."

Garrett blinked once, then focused on Pestilence. He inhaled deeply once, before a slow, predatory smile curved his lips. His eyes hazed to red, and he licked his lips.

"Good idea, love."

CHAPTER SIX

While Garrett hadn't experienced desire for anyone other than Aiden in nearly three years, there was no denying the burning need he felt for Pestilence. He wanted to peel those breeches down his long legs. His mouth watered to suck his cock and balls.

Growling under his breath, Garrett kicked the blanket from him. His nakedness surprised him, but not enough to make him pause. He swung his legs over the side and rose.

When they'd left the hospital, Pestilence had warned Garrett that he would pass out upon traveling through the mists. He wasn't alarmed to wake in a strange room. As he stalked toward his soon-to-be lover, he barely gave the lavish surroundings a second look.

By the time Garrett reached Pestilence, the horseman had gained his feet. The man tried to straighten fully, but his back seemed to have a slightly permanent hunch to it. That left them almost at eye level with each other.

Perfect for kissing.

Garrett cupped Pestilence's jaw and took possession of his mouth. The move must have taken the man by surprise, for he gasped and tensed. Taking advantage, he thrust his tongue in and began to explore.

Resting his hand on Pestilence's hip, Garrett pulled the tunic from the waistband of his horseman's belt. When he pushed his palm under the soft fabric, his light callouses caught a little on Pestilence's silky-smooth skin.

To Garrett's pleasure, Pestilence moaned and pushed into

his touch. He broke the kiss and grabbed the hem of his shirt. Tugging upward, Garrett grinned widely as he pulled it from the man.

"Oh, such beautiful skin," Garrett crooned as he took in Pestilence's pale flesh. There was just a hint of pink around his beaded nipples, and he bent to get a taste.

Just as Garrett licked over Pestilence's hard bud, drawing a gasp from the horseman, he heard Aiden order, "Bring him here, Garrett."

After a quick suck on Pestilence's nipple, Garrett straightened. He grinned as he admired the flush on his new lover's neck and face. His amber eyes had darkened nearly to gold.

Gorgeous.

Taking Pestilence's hand, Garrett turned and began leading him toward the bed. He took in Aiden's sprawled form and groaned. His human — *finally, he's mine* — already had his legs spread, and he worked two fingers in and out of his ass.

"Please tell me you have lube handy," Garrett rumbled, squeezing Pestilence's hand. "It's been a long time for me, and I'm gonna need plenty to take your long dick."

Pestilence's eyes dilated even more as he dipped his chin in a quick nod. "Here." He crossed to his nightstand and opened a drawer.

"Excellent." Garrett snagged the tube and held it out to Aiden. "Finish getting yourself ready for me, sweetheart, while I finish stripping Pestilence."

Aiden took the lubricant with a grin. "Oh, yeah. I wanna see all that pale skin." As he spoke, he rolled to his side, lifted one leg, and popped the cap on the tube.

Garrett chuckled as he winked at Aiden. He knew his lover enjoyed a little strip-tease while he fingered his own ass. Instead of it being him, he would give him Pestilence to eyeball.

"You wanna see the rest of Pestilence's gorgeous body, Aiden?" Garrett asked gruffly, smirking at his human. "How badly?"

While pouring slick onto his fingers, Aiden licked his lips. "So, so much," he whispered huskily. He set the tube on the comforter, then propped his head in his hand. "I want to see Pestilence's erection. I know it's gonna sink so deep in me."

Aiden thrust one slick finger into his channel before quickly sliding in a second. His muscle stretched around his fingers, and he nibbled his bottom lip. He swept his gaze over Pestilence, heat filling his eyes.

Garrett positioned Pestilence beside the bed, standing at his back. Wrapping his arms around the horseman's waist, he palmed the man's chest, using his fingertips to tease his nipples. He moved the other down and palmed Pestilence's thigh, sliding his thumb along his erection.

Pestilence trembled in his hold.

"Look at Aiden's hole stretching for his fingers," Garrett purred into Pestilence's ear as he continued to tease the tip of his thumb along his breeches-covered length. "Do you want to slide your long boner deep in there?"

Groaning, Pestilence gripped his wrists and shuddered. "Yessss," he hissed. "Been too long. Need it."

"How long is too long, Pestilence?" Garrett asked curiously before licking along the curve of the horseman's pointed ear.

"A-About three centuries," Pestilence replied breathily.

Garrett met Aiden's gaze over Pestilence's shoulder. He grinned at his human, knowing he was thinking the same thing.

We are gonna make our new lover feel sooooo good.

"Then let's get this party started," Garrett whispered. "Another finger, Aiden," he ordered as he gripped the buckle on Pestilence's thin belt. "I'm in you first, with Pestilence in me. Then we're gonna switch."

"Yes!" Aiden cried, shoving in a third digit.

To Garrett's pleasure, Pestilence didn't counter him. Instead, he groaned and gripped the waist of his breeches, pushing. His need made him a little uncoordinated, and Garrett found his fumbling . . . endearing.

Of course, if I'd gone that long without sex, I'd be out of my head, too.

Considering his own cock throbbed and twitched at his groin, Garrett knew it wouldn't be long until he needed to give in to his own desires.

Garrett made quick work of Pestilence's belt and tie-fly. The flaps immediately separated, his lover's slender erection thrusting between them. As Garrett's chute clenched in anticipation, he gripped the length and gave it a leisurely stroke.

"Oh, Pest," Aiden whined. "You'll go so deep."

Aiden's words were true. As Garrett pushed Pestilence's breeches down his long legs, he realized his new lover's erection had to be a foot long. His own nine-inch shaft had a bit more girth to it, and he knew his lover would enjoy their differences.

Dropping to one knee, Garrett tapped Pestilence's calf. "Lift."

Pestilence peered down at him with a lust-drunk gaze. Then he must have realized what Garrett meant. He picked up one foot, then the other, allowing Garrett to peel the form-fitting pants from him.

"Roll onto your back, and spread your legs, Aiden," Garrett ordered while rising back to his feet. Once his human had obeyed, he gripped Pestilence's hips. "Onto the bed between his legs."

Even as Pestilence obeyed, he asked, "I thought I was fucking you first."

Garrett grinned as he climbed onto the bed, too. "You are." Seeing the horseman's questioning look, he waggled his eyebrows. "While Aiden gets me ready" —he spread his legs, positioning his knees on either side of Aiden's shoulders, facing Pestilence—"I'm going to suck your dick until you come, then get you hard again."

Pestilence groaned, gripping the base of his erection in one long-fingered hand. "D-Don't think I could soften, anyway." Meeting Garrett's gaze, he pinned him with a feral expression. "Not until all our bonding is complete, anyway."

Returning Pestilence's feral grin with one his own, Garrett rumbled, "Good."

As Garrett leaned forward and opened his mouth, he felt Aiden's finger gently rub his opening. He instinctively clenched, but as he wrapped his lips around Pestilence's crown, he forced himself to relax. Resting one hand on the bed and the other on his horseman's hip, he took in more of the man's erection.

Pestilence's flavor burst across Garrett's tongue. The horseman tasted an odd mixture of musky and sweet. Garrett inhaled deeply as he took in more, relishing the slight flavor of Pestilence's pre-cum.

Reveling in the sound of Pestilence's moan as well as the way he cradled his head, Garrett began a hard sucking rhythm. He felt the shudder that worked through his new lover's body and lost himself in the feel of the smooth flesh in his mouth. His own cock twitched in time with the beat of the thick vein running along the underside of Pestilence's shaft.

Garrett wanted to sink his fangs into that vein in the worst way, but he wasn't at a good angle for it.

Another time.

Just as Pestilence began rocking his hips, his rhythm jerky and unsteady, Garrett registered the stretch in his ass. The mild burn eased his need to come. The pheromones pouring off his lovers and their delicious flavors of arousal kept him from softening.

Just as the sting eased, Garrett heard Pestilence shout. His mouth was filled with his new lover's salty, bitter essence. He swallowed quickly, only to have the horseman give him more.

Garrett swallowed it all, continuing to suck lightly, keeping Pestilence stimulated. While he probably wouldn't have needed to, he couldn't resist. He enjoyed sucking cock, and he was good at it, having been told many times over the centuries.

"Oh, fuck, Garrett," Pestilence muttered. "You look fantastic sucking my cock."

"It'll look even better sinking into his ass," Aiden claimed before smacking Garrett on said ass. "Turn around. I need you in me, and you're ready."

With a husky chuckle, Garrett popped off Pestilence's length. He reached up and gripped the horseman's nape, then pulled him into a short, hard kiss. After sharing the taste of Pestilence's release with the man, Garrett let go and swiftly turned around.

As soon as Garrett was positioned between the two men, Aiden reached forward and gripped his dick. He groaned, and it was his turn to shudder. Watching his human, he enjoyed the sight and feel of him slicking up his erection.

Garrett felt his balls begin to tighten, so he grabbed Aiden's wrist. "Enough," he panted. "Need you now." Garrett peered over his shoulder at Pestilence. "Both of you."

To Garrett's surprise, he realized how true that was, too. He felt the faint bond between both men, and he craved deepening it. That connection seemed like the most important thing in the world right then.

Pestilence gripped Garrett's hip with one hand and pressed between his shoulder blades with the other. With a hungry smile, he told him, "Slide into our Aiden, Garrett, so I may take you."

More than on board with that, Garrett did as he was told. He turned his focus back to Aiden and levered over him. Even though he'd fucked his human many times over the years, as he guided his erection to his hole, it somehow felt brand new all over again.

"Aiden," Garrett whispered huskily, smiling at him. "Love you."

"Love you, too." Aiden smiled back at him, his emotions shining in his eyes. "Now, fuck me."

Chuckling huskily, Garrett pushed. His dick sank smooth and easy into Aiden's well-lubed hole. He groaned upon feeling the hot, exquisite cocoon.

Garrett bottomed out and stilled, goose bumps breaking out on his arms. Threading his fingers through Aiden's hair, he lowered his face and pressed a light kiss to his human's lips. Then he peered over his shoulder and met Pestilence's heated gaze.

"Take me," Garrett ordered. "I can't keep still much longer."

Pestilence grinned, showing off plenty of pointed teeth. "Mine."

As Garrett felt his chute open to the horseman's long, slender prick, he let out a sigh and did his best to relax.

Aiden touched his jaw, gaining his attention. He grinned and licked his lips. "Let me taste the other man we'll soon learn to love. I bet he lingers on your tongue."

Groaning, Garrett sealed his mouth over Aiden's and gave his human what he wanted. He licked into his lover's mouth, allowing him to taste Pestilence on his tongue. Sweat beaded on his skin as he struggled to keep his hips still and his body relaxed.

Garrett could barely believe that Pestilence had gone along with his plan. His dick twitched within Aiden as he anticipated fucking the horseman. He didn't deserve that kind of trust.

"Stop thinking like that," Pestilence snarled, bumping his balls against Garrett's. "You're mine. You're both mine, and we trust you."

Yanking his mouth from Aiden's, Garrett turned and met Pestilence's narrowed eyes.

His new lover tapped his temple.

"We are linked, you and I." Pestilence lowered his head and pecked an awkward kiss to his lips. "Those thoughts do not belong in our bedroom."

Even as pleasure burst through Garrett's rectum, his face heated with embarrassment. "Right." He hadn't realized a mind link would form with Pestilence.

"Now." Pestilence ease partway out of Garrett's body. "Fuck your chosen beloveds."

Garrett moaned roughly and obeyed.

CHAPTER SEVEN

While Pestilence knew it wasn't the sexiest of topics, he hadn't been able to stand listening to Garrett's self-doubts a second longer. He'd had to interrupt. Fortunately, it hadn't put too much of a damper on things.

As Garrett began to move, pushing back against him and taking his cock, then thrusting forward to sink back into Aiden, Pestilence's mind began to shut down. He knew the conversation wasn't over, but right then, nothing mattered except pleasing and connecting with his chosens.

"That's it," Pestilence growled, heat sparking up his spine. He gripped Garrett's hips with both hands and moved with his vampire. "Your hole stretches so pretty."

Pestilence listened to Garrett's groan and grinned. He couldn't help but stare at where he penetrated the man. His chosen vampire taking him into his body truly was a gorgeous sight.

"Oh, gods," Aiden moaned, drawing Pestilence's attention. "Yes! Right there."

Hissing as his cock throbbed, Pestilence peered over Garrett's shoulder. The vampire had torn his lips away from their human and buried his face in his neck. Aiden's neck was arched, his face appeared flushed, and a look of delirious pleasure was etched across his features.

In the next instant, Pestilence scented the delicious aroma of Aiden's seed. He groaned, gritting his teeth as his own balls lifted. When the smell of Aiden's blood perfumed the air, telling Pestilence that Garrett had bitten their human, he lost it.

Pestilence's testicles pulled tight, and his orgasm crashed through him. He buried himself deep, forcing Garrett to do the same. The vampire didn't seem to mind, his body shaking and his chute rippling.

Roaring with pleasure, Pestilence floated on the heady knowledge that he'd satisfied his chosen vampire. He needed more . . . he needed it all. Pestilence bent over Garrett and sank his pointed teeth deep into the flesh where his neck met his shoulder.

Garrett tipped his head back and howled.

Even as Pestilence sucked on the wound, wiping his tongue over the torn flesh over and over, he felt his vampire buck beneath him. The whimpering cries as he shuddered would have concerned him . . . except for the renewed smell of arousal. The clutching ripple around his pulsing erection reassured him, too.

He'd caused his chosen vampire to come again.

Smugness filling him, Pestilence eased his teeth free. He licked over the wound, liking the large scar that formed. His heart thudded wildly upon seeing the proof that Garrett accepted their bond, accepted him.

I'll do my best to keep him happy for always.

Looking over his shoulder, Garrett met his gaze. *That goes both ways, you know. Partners please each other.*

Pestilence smiled upon hearing Garrett's voice in his head. It felt so damn intimate. *I'm ancient and still have something new to learn.*

Garrett grinned, then winked. "You ready to ease out of me?" he asked. Then he turned his head and drew his attention to Aiden, who was staring up at them both with a heavy-lidded gaze. "I don't know about you, but I'm not passed out from pleasure, yet."

Holding Aiden's gaze, Pestilence did his best to tease. "Well, we wouldn't want to disappoint Garrett, would we, sweet chosen?"

Aiden snickered. "Definitely not." He reached beyond Garrett and rested his hand on Pestilence's shoulder, giving it a squeeze. "Ya better move, so we can please our vampire."

As Garrett barked a laugh, Pestilence did as he'd been bid, letting out a chuckle of his own. "Our chosen's wish and all that."

"So, how do you want me?" Aiden asked around a gasp. "Oh, damn. I'm leaking."

Pestilence watched Garrett move out from between them, so he peered down. A primal surge of possessiveness rolled through him. He had the desire to slide his still hard shaft into his human's opening and mix his own seed with Garrett's.

Gods, where are these urges coming from?

When Pestilence had agreed to forge a bond with a pair to be his chosen companions, never would he have guessed he would feel like this.

Touching Aiden's most intimate place, Pestilence rubbed Garrett's seed into his opening. He wanted in there . . . desperately. "Any way I can get you," he whispered, absently answering Aiden's earlier question.

Aiden's vibrant green eyes widened, and he nibbled his bottom lip. Somehow, his cheeks flushed a little more. He even wriggled his hips, as if in invitation.

Garrett wrapped his arm around Pestilence's shoulder, nuzzling the crook of his shoulder. "I know how I want to see you together," he crooned into his ear.

The fine hairs on Pestilence's nape stood on end. His cock twitched, eager to play in any way his chosen offered. He hadn't had sex in so long, but he couldn't remember it being so much fun, either.

Pestilence turned his head and pecked a kiss to Garrett's lips, licking into his mouth for a few seconds. "How would you like to watch us?" he asked roughly even as he continued to tease at Aiden's opening, dipping his fingertips in and out of the warm, loose muscle.

"Lie on your back," Garrett ordered, rubbing his back. "Aiden will ride you while I fuck you."

"H-How will that work?" Aiden sounded confused, but he started moving, pulling away from Pestilence's touch.

Garrett's grin appeared feral. "Trust me." He pointed. "Hand me the lube."

Nodding, Pestilence obeyed. While Aiden rolled to his knees and handed Garrett the lube, Pestilence sprawled onto his back. He arched one brow when his chosen vampire pulled him forward, drawing his ass to the edge of the bed.

After taking the lube, Garrett helped Aiden straddle Pestilence's waist. "Take him in, sweetheart," he crooned into their human's ear. "Sink down and ride him slow and easy while I open him up."

Nibbling his lip, Aiden nodded.

Pestilence groaned as he stared between them.

Garrett poured slick onto his right hand, then closed the tube and tossed it aside. With his now-free left hand, he grabbed Pestilence's erection and pointed it upward. As Aiden touched his hole to the head of his dick, Garrett began massaging his opening.

Breathing deeply, Pestilence did his best not to clench . . . and tremble. Aiden's body opened, encasing his crown in gripping heat, and sweat beaded on his skin. As Garrett pushed a long finger into his chute, Aiden lowered onto his cock.

The feel of the human surrounding him felt different than the vampire—not better or worse, just different. His silky walls milked him eagerly. His channel already held plenty of moisture that made moving in and out easy.

As Aiden rested his hands on Pestilence's chest and began fucking himself on his cock, his human groaned low and needy. He tipped his head back, and his smile appeared almost loopy. Aiden's movements were slow and languorous as he raised and lowered himself on Pestilence's dick, looking for all the world as if he never wanted to be anywhere ever again.

"Aiden," Pestilence rumbled, resting his hands on Aiden's hips. "So good. So beautiful. Gods." He didn't try to control his sweet human's movements, just held him. "Feel so fantastic."

Opening his eyes, Aiden peered down at him. He smiled, the expression one of feral intensity. "You reach so deep, Pest," he murmured with a hum. "So very deep." Settling his ass against Pestilence's groin, he wriggled, as if relishing feeling his prick embedded within him. "Love it."

While Pestilence recognized the fact that Garrett was opening his ass, he couldn't focus on it. Instead, all he could do was stare in wonder at Aiden. He figured that had been Garrett's intention.

Whatever. It worked.

Pestilence watched as Aiden's short, thick dick bobbed from his shaved groin. He admired the lines of muscle in his arms and chest. The beads of sweat gliding down Aiden's temples, neck, and chest begged to be licked . . . as did the precum drooling from his slit.

His mouth watered, and he groaned.

Sliding his arms up and around Aiden's back, Pestilence drew his chosen human to him. He slid his arm up his back to cradle his neck. Clenching his gut, he rocked up and captured Aiden's mouth.

"Gods, such a perfect sight," Garrett rumbled, his voice husky and deep. "Keep kissing. Gonna fuck you now and make you spill in Aiden."

Pestilence moaned into Aiden's mouth. He didn't fight it when Garrett moved his feet wider, propping them on the edge of the bed. He continued to urge Aiden to rise and fall on his dick until he felt something pop past his opening.

Breaking the kiss, Pestilence sucked in a surprised gasp. He tensed. While it didn't truly hurt, it felt . . . odd.

"Relax," Aiden urged, petting his face. He threaded his fingers through Pestilence's hair, tugging lightly. "So silky and smooth, just like I thought." His green eyes remained dark with pleasure as he rocked backward and took Pestilence to the root again. Aiden sighed. "Gods, you're long. Feel you in my throat."

Garrett chuckled roughly, peering over Aiden's shoulder. His deep brown eyes held a mixture of mirth and lust. "Like it deep, sweetheart?"

Aiden rested against Garrett and peered over his shoulder at him. "You're thicker. Stretch me more." He hummed and wriggled on Pestilence's prick. "Love how you both feel."

Pestilence suddenly realized that Garrett had stopped moving . . . because he was embedded fully inside him. The stretch didn't hurt, and the way the vampire rocked just a smidge to tease his prostate sent fiery tendrils through his groin. His chosen vampire wasn't kidding about fucking him into spilling in Aiden.

Moaning roughly, Pestilence clenched around Garrett's erection. He then popped his hips up a little, searching for friction on his throbbing shaft. Aiden rocked forward, returning his hands to Pestilence's chest, sliding his palms over his pectorals.

Feeling Aiden flick his nipples, Pestilence groaned and bucked again.

"Relax, Pestilence," Garrett urged. "Let us pleasure you." He rested one hand on Pestilence's hip and the other on Aiden's side. "Ride him, Aiden. Our lover needs it."

"Yessss," Aiden muttered, beginning to move much more swiftly than before. "Love fucking myself on your dick."

While Pestilence could have broken Garrett's hold on his hip, he didn't. He allowed his chosen vampire to lead . . . and it felt exquisite. The view was a damn amazing sight, too.

Aiden bounced on his dick, his expression eager and blissed-out. His prick bobbed before him, drooling pre-cum. Each bounce drew the most erotic moans and whimpers from Aiden's kiss-swollen lips.

When Pestilence peered over Aiden's shoulder, he spotted Garrett's feral expression. His vampire's eyes were blood red, and his lips were peeled back from his lips. Best of all was the look of adoration etched across his features . . . and it wasn't directed only at Aiden.

Garrett glanced between Aiden and Pestilence, his gaze sweeping over them both. He was licking his lips and grunting and huffing roughly. His body rocked as he slammed into Pestilence over and over.

On every second or third stroke, Garrett nailed Pestilence's prostate.

Between the beauty bouncing on his dick and the continued stimulation to his pleasure button, Pestilence knew he wasn't going to last . . . at all. His balls pulled tight again, and a fresh orgasmic wave rolled over his system. As he poured his essence into Aiden's body, he clenched rhythmically on Garrett's erection.

Hearing Garrett's bark of pleasure and feeling his heat warm him from the inside out, Pestilence moaned.

I could get used to that.

As soon as Garrett sank his fangs into Aiden's neck, Pestilence grabbed them both and pulled them to him. He opened his mouth and sank his sharp teeth into his human's flesh. As he drank his lover's iron-rich, life-giving fluid, Pestilence felt their bond snap into place, complete and unbreakable.

I'll make certain it ends up being for all time.

Pestilence couldn't imagine his life without these two men in it . . . even after such a short time.

CHAPTER EIGHT

Waking once more, Aiden smiled as he blinked open his eyes. He glanced left and right, admiring the men on either side of him. Facing Pestilence on his right, Aiden was partially draped over him, his head on his shoulder. His backside was being warmed by Garrett, who was snuggled against him.

"Welcome back, sweet chosen," Pestilence murmured softly. He rubbed his fingers through Aiden's hair, pushing the damp locks from his face. "Thank you for choosing to live, for choosing me."

"Thank you for giving me Garrett," Aiden whispered, smiling up at Pestilence. Lifting his arm, he traced over the horseman's thin lips. "For saving me."

"I'm sorry you needed saving." Garrett's deep voice sounded behind him, rough from sleep. Scraping his teeth along Aiden's shoulder, he muttered, "I should have gotten to you sooner. Gods, Aiden. I almost lost you."

Aiden turned a little, frowning at Garrett. "And if I had yelled for you as soon as the vampire walked in and spoke, this wouldn't have happened, either," he pointed out. Rubbing his hand over Garrett's shoulder and up his neck, he squeezed lightly, trying to soothe his vampire. "I froze, so technically, it's my fault."

Pestilence sighed deeply, his long arms reaching around them both. "Technically, it's the rogue vampire's fault," he pointed out before pressing a kiss to Aiden's temple. Then he levered up on his elbow and leaned over him to press a swift kiss to Garrett's temple. As Pestilence settled against Aiden's side, he propped his head on his hand, his expression serious. "Human or paranormal, the skein of your life is weaved by the Moirai. You're born, you live, and you die. When it's time for your life-strand to be cut, no one can stop that."

Aiden gaped for an instant, then snickered. "Uh, you did."

Chuckling, Pestilence smiled at him. "In reality, I pulled you out of the tapestry altogether, so you're no longer bound by the Moirai."

"Why?" Aiden asked curiously. "Why would you bother?"

Pestilence hummed as he swept his gaze down Aiden's body, then over to Garrett's and back up his. "Why save a stranger?" His smile turned heated as he winked. "You ask that after we've bonded and are lying in bed together?"

Aiden relaxed on the pillow between them, surprised at how comfortable he felt lying naked between the two men. With their heat warming him, he didn't even need a blanket. Still, he couldn't help resting one hand on his rounded belly.

"I am curious myself," Garrett added softly with furrowed brows. "You owed us nothing. What if it turns out we're not compatible?"

"That's a risk in any relationship," Pestilence reminded them before sighing deeply. He eased to a sitting position. "I suppose we all have baggage."

Aiden followed his example and eased to a sitting position, moving beside him with his back against the headboard. He felt his chute muscles twinge. To his surprise, however, he didn't feel dirty.

"One of you cleaned me," Aiden blurted out. Feeling his cheeks heat, he wrapped his arms around himself in embarrassment. "Uh, sorry I passed out."

Pestilence chuckled as he wrapped his arms around Aiden on one side. Garrett slotted up on his other side. Then they threaded their fingers together over Aiden's arms.

"I love that we gave you so much pleasure that you passed out, Aiden," Pestilence told him, surprising Aiden with an eyebrow waggle and a smirk. "Since I hadn't had sex in centuries, it was a great boost to my ego."

"Is that why you chose us?" Garrett asked, squeezing their twined fingers. "For sex?"

Shrugging, Pestilence told them, "Not *just* sex. Over the last couple of years, I watched a couple of my brothers find chosen companions." His pale cheeks took on a pinkish hue, and he cleared his throat. "While I have hundreds of demons living and working at the estate, they are like my children. I feel no attraction to them."

"You were lonely," Aiden murmured, understanding. He smiled up at Pestilence, who appeared so very uncomfortable. "You wanted friends. Someone to care for, and who would care for you."

Pestilence nodded once. "I did."

Garrett licked his lips, his expression turning thoughtful. "So, what drew you to us?"

"Well." The pink on Pestilence's face darkened. "I asked Death to keep an eye out for me. Um, for a couple facing separation, who might be willing to accept the love of a third in order to stay together." After clearing his throat, Pestilence added, "I really don't know how he settled on you, but I trust my brother enough that he'd choose someone compatible."

Aiden's mind reeled. Pestilence had asked his brother, and Death had chosen them. Aiden wondered what criteria the other horseman had used. Then he realized it didn't really matter.

"Well, thank you," Aiden stated. Smiling at Pestilence, taking in his worried expression, he bumped his shoulder into the other man's upper arm. "Regardless of how Death chose, I'm grateful." Another thought occurred, and he glanced down at himself. "I hope you're not disappointed."

Garrett growled, obviously guessing where his mind had gone. While rubbing their twined fingers over Aiden's slightly rounded belly, he grumbled, "There's nothing wrong with your body, sweetheart. I wish you'd believe me."

Pestilence evidently caught on, for he cocked his head and stated, "I enjoy your softness, Aiden." Then he met Garrett's gaze. "Just as I enjoy Garrett's hard muscles. You're different. Unique." Pestilence refocused on Aiden's face, his amber eyes lighting up with renewed heat. "I can't wait to take my time exploring you both. I—"

Pausing, Pestilence tipped his head to the side. A wince twisted his features. He closed his eyes and rested the back of his head against the headboard as he began a series of slow inhalations.

"Pest?" Aiden asked tentatively. He exchanged a look with Garrett. Untangling one arm, he rubbed a hand over Pestilence's side. "Are you okay?" Considering the horseman's expression, Aiden decided that was a ridiculous question, so he tried again. "What's wrong?"

Garrett used the hand he had behind Aiden to grip Pestilence's shoulder. "How can we help?"

A slight smile eased Pestilence's contorted expression. "Just being here helps," he whispered. Opening his eyes, he glanced between them. "I just lost a demon."

"Lost a—" Garrett began, then snapped his mouth shut. He rubbed over his shoulder. "I'm sorry."

"That's horrible," Aiden murmured, knowing he was just as confused as Garrett. Disentangling himself from between the men, he eased around Pestilence and settled on his other side. "Um, how do you know?" Aiden asked, cuddling up to the horseman.

To Aiden's relief, Garrett immediately eased into Aiden's prior position. He wrapped around Pestilence, too. They both rubbed their hands over their horseman's chest, attempting to soothe him.

Pestilence's tense body relaxed under their ministrations. "A horseman is connected with their demons. Not on the same level as I am with you," he told them, trying to clarify. "When one is killed, I feel the thread snap."

"Oh, wow," Aiden murmured, unable to fathom it. "Does it hurt much?"

Grimacing, Pestilence shook his head. "It's not so much painful as . . . saddening." Then he smiled faintly at them. "Thank you for your comfort."

"Of course," Garrett rumbled, sliding his hand up to cup Pestilence's jaw. "Anytime."

"Always," Aiden added.

Then Garrett leaned forward and captured Pestilence's lips. He watched the vampire slide his tongue into the other man's mouth. His lips teased and massaged the horseman's.

Aiden's heart sped up, and blood flowed south. A couple of days ago, if anyone had told him he would watch his lover of nearly three years make out with another and not feel jealous, he would have never believed it. He certainly would never had thought he would get turned on by it.

But I am. Damn, that's hawt.

Unable to help himself, Aiden reached down and touched his plumping dick lightly. He moved his penis to a more comfortable position. Even that light stimulation caused him to thicken even more.

When Garrett broke the kiss, he chuckled huskily. "I'd meant that to be a soothing kiss." His eyes had begun to bleed to red as he turned his attention to Aiden while still petting Pestilence's jaw. "Not start another round, but damn, you always smell so good, sweetheart."

Pestilence's nostrils flared, and he reached out to Aiden. "He's so right," he muttered, cupping his jaw and pulling away from Garrett. "Come here."

Aiden went eagerly.

Just before Pestilence sealed his lips to Aiden's, he groaned. "Shit, I can't do this right now." He pecked a kiss to Aiden's lips, then rested their foreheads together. "I'm sorry, sweetheart. I need to go."

Disappointment filled Aiden, and he couldn't help the whine in his voice when he asked, "You do? Why?"

Pestilence pecked Aiden's lips again, then drew away a little. After glancing at Garrett, he explained, "With Diderman deceased, I need to find out if he completed his task." After swiping his thumb along Aiden's jaw, Pestilence released him. "If not, I must assign another demon to complete it right away."

As disappointed as Aiden felt, he nodded. "Duty calls. I get it." Slipping from the bed, he asked, "How do you know it's Diderman? More of that connection thingy?" Walking away from the bed, Aiden peered around the room. "Um. Do I have any clothes here?"

I came in a hospital gown, right?

"Yes. More of that connection thingy," Pestilence told him, sounding amused. "I had a couple of my demons fetch clothes that should fit you. Garrett, too." He beckoned as he walked to a large wardrobe, then threw open the doors. "Feel free to go through anything. This is your home now."

"My home?" Aiden murmured as he began opening and closing drawers and cupboards. "Will I have a chance to get anything from the coven?"

Garrett rested his hand on Aiden's shoulder, rubbing lightly. "The coven isn't safe, Aiden," he told him.

Suddenly, Aiden recalled Garrett's injuries in the hospital room before his freak-out. "Did someone at the coven do that to you?" When Garrett nodded, Aiden gasped. "Why?"

Standing there naked in Pestilence's opulent bedroom, Garrett explained what had happened between him and his coven.

Fear slithered up Aiden's spine. "Th-They were going t-to

wipe my mind?" A tremble worked through him, and he wrapped his arms tight around himself. "I-I can never go back."

Two pairs of arms wrapped around Aiden. He leaned into the embraces of his lovers, taking comfort. Resting his temple against Garrett's familiar, broad pectoral, he offered Pestilence a thankful smile.

Pestilence smiled back, looking reassuring. "By bonding with me, you will never have to worry about a vampire's mental manipulation abilities again."

Gaping, Aiden stared up at the horseman. "Really?"

With a wink and a nod, Pestilence stated, "Yes, and you will also be able to communicate with us both telepathically, just as a standard vampire beloved would."

Aiden squealed with delight and shimmied a dance within their arms. "Thank you!" He threw his arms around Pestilence's waist and wriggled a little more. Upon hearing both men's chuckles, Aiden got ahold of himself, although he couldn't stop grinning. "When will that develop?"

Then Aiden squinted and stared hard at Pestilence. *Can you hear me now?*

Pestilence's brows shot up, and he rubbed at his temple.

"That would be shouting, sweetheart," Garrett told him, chuckling. "I'll teach you." Easing Aiden out of Pestilence's arms, he added, "Didn't you need to do something?"

Grimacing, Pestilence nodded, and he stepped away. "Right."

Aiden finally noticed that Pestilence had already donned the clothes Garrett had removed . . . however long ago that was.

"Wait," Aiden cried. "Can we come?" He glanced at Garrett before refocusing on Pestilence. "Can we see your . . . home?"

They wouldn't be expected to stay in the bedroom all the time, right?

Pestilence appeared surprised, but pleased. "Of course." He waved toward the wardrobe. "Dress quickly, sweet chosen." Smiling at Garrett, Pestilence added, "You are both welcome to join me or to simply explore."

Grinning, Aiden quickly found some clothes and yanked them on.

CHAPTER NINE

Garrett peered around his new home with interest. To his surprise, Pestilence had set up his realm as a sprawling estate. Unbonded demons lived in one of several wings in their own suite. Bonded demons were given a cottage on the back property, built to their specifications.

There were ten large barn-like structures, but Pestilence explained they held training equipment—anything from fighting pits to educational centers. The demons had to learn not only how to spar but how to live in the human realm. They were taught how to use their magick, allowing them to hide their true features.

Watching Pestilence direct another demon to finish Diderman's assignment, Garrett felt a niggle of unease. He'd heard that the demon had been assigned the task of spreading a respiratory infection in a nursing home. It wasn't the disease that bothered Garrett. He understood that it was their duty. Instead, Garrett didn't like the fact that the nursing home was located in Philadelphia.

"I've been expecting Diderman's death for a while," Pestilence commented after the demon who was charged with finishing his assignment had left. Sitting in a large chair, he rubbed the back of his neck.

Aiden leaned his hip against Pestilence's armrest. "Really?"

Pestilence nodded as he wrapped his arms around Aiden. Drawing him onto his lap, he told them, "Diderman was over four hundred years old, but he still acted like he was under a century." He sighed as he shook his head. "The demon enjoyed getting into mischief a little too much, so the fact that he found himself on the wrong side of another paranormal or magick user doesn't surprise me."

As Aiden pressed kisses along the underside of Pestilence neck, Garrett smiled and rounded the desk. He watched the horseman sigh and tip his head back. Taking advantage, Garrett threaded his fingers through Pestilence's hair and massaged his scalp.

Humming, Pestilence relaxed under their ministration.

"Wow," Pestilence murmured, a look of pure bliss on his features. "And you were worried we weren't compatible."

Garrett chuckled, smirking. "So, we're living here." He didn't wait for confirmation. Instead, he asked, "Do we have jobs? Can we help in some way?"

As far as Garrett had seen, everything ran like a well-oiled machine.

"Well, you were a guard at your coven," Pestilence began slowly. "Not much call for that here." His smile held a wealth of concern. "Do you have any hobbies you'd be interested in focusing on? There's no need to earn money here or anything."

"Can I train with your demons?" Garrett asked, cocking his head. "I can't imagine sitting on my ass all day."

Aiden straightened on Pestilence's lap, snickering. "Yeah. You'd go stir-crazy in no time."

Garrett nodded, grimacing. "Afraid so."

Pestilence hummed. "If you're working out with the demons, I'll need to assign one of my older ones to you, so you know who'd be a fair competition." The horseman must have scented Garrett's confusion, for he told him, "Once everyone knows who you are, none of my demons would try to hurt you on purpose. With that said, the older a demon becomes, the more powerful he becomes." He stared at Garrett earnestly. "I would never want you injured by accident."

Holding Pestilence's gaze, Garrett nodded in understanding. "I'll give it some thought." Then another idea formed, and he commented, "You know, over a hundred and fifty years ago, I worked as a blacksmith for our coven." Garrett winked. "Who shoes you and your brothers' horses?"

Chuckling, Pestilence grinned at him. "Our horses are magickally bound to us, so no shoes and no hoof trimming." Cocking his head, he narrowed his eyes. "However, if you were a blacksmith, I bet you occasionally made weapons. You could dabble in our forge, making blades and such for my demons."

Garrett grinned, excitement filling him. "Nice!"

Pestilence focused on Aiden. "What about you, sweet chosen?"

Aiden snickered, his green eyes shining. "Would my *Kindle* work in this realm?"

Barking a laugh, Garrett drew Pestilence's attention. He grinned at their new lover. "If *Kindle* works here, Garrett would very happily sit around all day reading and eating gumdrops."

"Love to read, do you?" Pestilence focused on Aiden with a smile. After their human smiled, he asked, "What are gumdrops?"

Garrett laughed again. "When we slip into the coven to get our things, we'll stop somewhere and get some." Then he sobered. "Oh, I guess you never did say if we could sneak in and out of there."

Oh, well. It's just stuff. I would have liked to say good-bye to a few of my friends, though.

Pestilence hummed softly. "I can get you in and out without anyone knowing . . . unless there's surveillance in your individual rooms."

"You know, if I had a phone," Garrett began, thinking

68

quickly. "I could contact Daniel or Tristan. They would bring us some of our stuff, if I asked."

"Do you trust them?" Pestilence asked curiously.

Garrett nodded. "We grew up together. They've been my best friends for nearly two hundred years."

"You're gonna miss them, huh?" Aiden murmured, reaching over the back of the chair and grabbing his wrist.

"Yeah," Garrett admitted.

"But not for a few more centuries," Pestilence countered, smiling at him. "Ask them to change covens. Then they could hang with you whenever you wished." He shrugged his shoulder as his smile turned wry. "Well, within reason."

"You'd take us to the human realm to hang with them on occasion?" Garrett grinned. He hadn't thought of that. "And what do you mean, a few more centuries?"

Pestilence cleared his throat and shifted restlessly for a second. His cheeks took on a pinkish hue, and Garrett smelled his slight embarrassment.

"Hey, what's wrong?" Garrett asked, confused at Pestilence's reaction.

Meeting Garrett's gaze, Pestilence told him, "I'd hoped you intended to stay with me long term. That means, well" —he cleared his throat again—"forever."

"Forever?" Aiden squeaked. "How's that possible?"

Rubbing his hand up and down Aiden's back, Pestilence told him, "I was created by the gods when the realms were formed and humans and paranormals were born." He shrugged. "I've always been here, and I always will be."

"You can't die?" Aiden asked, clearly shocked.

Pestilence's eyebrows furrowed. "Yes, I can die, but the gods just bring me back."

"It's *happened*?" Garrett's gut clenched at that knowledge.

Holding up two fingers, Pestilence told them, "Over the

course of the many millennia I've been around, I've been de-capitated twice. Once by Death, and once by War."

"Holy shit," Aiden squeaked. "Why?"

While Pestilence's eyes held no malice — in fact, they danced with mirth — he told them, "We were at war with each other. We don't pull that shit anymore." He broke into laughter. "Damn, the gods were angry at us. Nothing like a goddess telling a group of fifteen-hundred-year-old creations that they're acting like children."

Garrett shook his head as he thrust his free hand through his own hair. "Damn. Which goddess was that?"

Pestilence appeared thoughtful. "Hmmm . . . Aphrodite."

"Ooookay," Aiden mumbled.

They both grinned at their human.

"Soooo," Garrett began, getting them back on track. "We're going to be around awhile. Huh?"

Donning a hopeful expression, Pestilence glanced between them. "I'd like that."

"So would we," Aiden claimed, answering for both of them.

Garrett nodded, surprised at how quickly he'd come to care for Pestilence.

Grinning, Pestilence pulled Aiden into a deep kiss.

Watching the pair, Garrett reached down and gripped his hardening cock behind the fly of his jeans. He suddenly knew exactly what Aiden must have felt a while ago. His lovers making out was damn hot.

Pestilence broke the kiss and groaned. "Can I give you all a tour later?" he asked, his soft tenor having turned gruff.

"Hell, yeah," Garrett confirmed, helping the pair to their feet.

After the tour a day later, Pestilence explained that human technology didn't work in the demon realm.

"No *Kindle*?" Aiden sighed dramatically. "I guess I'll have to read the old fashion way. I'll set up a PO box to have my books delivered to."

"Sorry, my sweet chosen," Pestilence rumbled, wrapping him up from behind. He pressed a kiss to his temple before murmuring, "I'll have a demon take you somewhere to order more and pick them up whenever you wish."

Aiden grinned over his shoulder at him, accepting a kiss in the process.

Garret chuckled at his lovers' antics. "So, think we'll pass out again when we pass through this?" They were heading toward the mists.

Pestilence released Aiden so they could start moving again. The horseman walked beside them, and a couple of demons trailed them. They had their own duties to perform, so once they reached the human realm, they would go their own way.

"Most likely," Pestilence admitted, glancing between them with a smile. "But it won't always be like that."

Garrett enjoyed seeing Pestilence smile. From the comments some of the demons made, he hadn't had much to smile about for . . . well, a long time. The demons appeared to like the change, too.

It seemed they appreciated seeing their master happy.

"Come here," Pestilence urged, wrapping an arm around each of their waists. "Let's go find a phone to call your friends."

"Ready," Aiden claimed.

After Garrett said the same, Pestilence did . . . something. His head swam, and black spots danced across his vision. He felt himself sway, then press heavily against a slender, wiry frame.

"You're okay," Pestilence crooned. "It'll pass quickly."

Garrett blinked once, twice. Then the spots began to clear.

His mind started to unfog, and he managed to get his feet under him.

"Wow," Garrett muttered, shaking his head. "That felt weird."

Straightening in Pestilence's hold, Garrett noticed Aiden was still out. His head rested on their horseman's chest, and his strong arm around his waist held him up. His expression appeared peaceful. Reaching over, Garrett rubbed his hand up and down Aiden's back.

"You weren't out long," Pestilence told him. While he eased his grip on Garrett, he didn't let him go. "Just a few seconds, really."

Garrett nodded. "Good." Glancing around, he recognized the area. "Secluded park. Nice."

Pestilence chuckled. "Can't have anyone seeing us pop in and out."

"Good point." Garrett focused on Aiden again. "How long do you think he'll be out?"

With a shrug, Pestilence explained, "It's different for everyone, although humans normally take longer to get used to it than paranormals."

Garrett hummed. "Well, want me to track down a phone while we wait for Aiden to rouse?"

"I don't want you far from me," Pestilence told him possessively, even as he released his waist. Then he bent and slid his free arm under Aiden's knees. "I'll follow you. We'll be invisible to everyone but you."

"Oh, am I immune to your glamour now, too?"

Pestilence nodded.

"Wow."

Garrett started forward, moving toward the jogging trails. If he was lucky, he could bum a phone off someone. Being a vampire, he could even force the issue if need be.

Fortunately, that didn't end up being the case.

Spotting a young woman jogging, Garrett waved and offered her a charming smile. "Hey, ma'am?" he called, seeing as she was wearing earbuds.

The lady paused and pulled them from her ears. "Hi." Openly perusing him, she asked, "Can I help you?"

Garrett heard Pestilence growl in his mind.

Relax. I'm yours. He gave his lover mental assurance.

Hell, yeah, you are.

Continuing to smile at the woman, Garrett easily convinced her to hand over her phone. He had to think a second before he recalled Daniel's phone number.

"Who is this?"

Garrett smirked upon hearing Daniel's non-greeting. "This is Garrett."

"Holy fuck! Garrett," Daniel barked. "Where the fuck have you been? Do you have any idea how much trouble you're in? Master Condor is pissed."

"Yeah, I figured as much. I need your help." Garrett hesitated, then stated, "But don't if it's going to get you into trouble with Condor."

"Fuck that," Daniel replied belligerently. "Whatever you need, me and Tristan are there for ya, buddy. What's up?"

Garrett explained what he and Aiden needed from their rooms and picked a time and place to meet.

"Can I reach you at this number?" Daniel asked as Garrett was saying good-bye.

"No. Sorry."

"I'll pick you up some burners."

After thanking Daniel once more, Garrett hung up and thanked the lady for her phone while handing it back to her.

CHAPTER TEN

Pestilence settled in the chair, glancing around the pub. He couldn't remember the last time he'd sat down for a meal in the human realm.

Bet that will change.

He couldn't say he minded.

"Hello, gentlemen. I'm Diana, and I'll be your waitress this evening." Diana glanced around at them all. Her gaze fell on Aiden, and she smiled a little wider. "Can I start you with some drinks or an appetizer?"

"Oh, yes, please," Aiden replied, smiling at her. "May I have a glass of your house merlot, please?"

"Good choice," Diana claimed, grinning. "What appetizer?"

Pestilence could tell Aiden was completely oblivious to the woman's attraction. Noticing the way Garrett reached over and took Aiden's hand while grabbing the appetizer card from the rack in the middle, he knew the vampire hadn't missed it, though. Smirking, Pestilence placed his own arm over the back of Aiden's chair and played with his shaggy, sandy-blond hair.

"Let's see what you have," Garrett commented, glancing over the card. It was the wine list side, and he tapped his forefinger on it. "They have *Troon's Druid Fluid*, sweetheart. Would you prefer that?"

Aiden's green eyes lit up. "Really?" He smiled at Diana. "Can I have that instead, please?"

Diana nodded, nibbling her bottom lip. "Of course."

Pestilence could scent her disappointment, but he couldn't give a shit.

Huh. Never been jealously possessive before. Interesting sensation.

"I'll take that house merlot," Pestilence told her. He didn't know anything about human wines, but if it had been good enough for Aiden, he would be happy to try it.

"Of course," Diana replied. She turned back to Garrett. "And for you, sir?"

Garrett hummed, then told her, "I'll take a bottle of *Amberbock*." As their waitress nodded, jotting on the pad, Garrett added, "And we'll take an order of your boneless hot wings, some potato skins, and jalapeno poppers."

Diana continued to nod and scribble.

Pestilence pointed at two men who'd walked through the front door a few seconds before. They'd been looking around and were now headed their way. He tensed as he asked, "Are those your friends, Garrett?"

Garrett looked in the direction he pointed and smiled. "Yeah." He released Aiden's hand and rose to his feet. "Hey, guys."

Gritting his teeth, Pestilence watched Garrett offer both men a hand-shake and hug.

He didn't realize he was growling until Aiden squeezed his thigh and spoke into his mind. *Stop it. They really are just friends. Never even fooled around together when they were younger.*

How do you know? Pestilence mentally winced at the irritation even in his mental voice.

Aiden laughed in his mind. *Ask him about it later.*

Pestilence unclenched his jaw and blew out a slow breath, calming his pulse.

"And what can I get you, gentlemen?" Diana asked after the men sat down.

The blond grabbed the card Garrett had left on the table. "Let's see."

Evidently, the light-brown haired vampire wasn't nearly so picky . . . or he'd been there before. "I'll take whatever *Michelob* you have on tap."

"Yeah, give me that, too," the other vampire said, tossing the card down. "Oh, hey, did you guys order appetizers?"

Garrett waggled his brows. "I took care of us."

"Good," the blond grunted. After the waitress left, he leaned forward and scowled at Garrett. "What the fuck, Gar?" he asked, keeping his voice low. "You ditch without even a word to either of us? What's going on?"

"First, Pestilence, this is Daniel and Tristan," Garrett introduced, pointing to the blond first. "Guys, these are my beloveds."

Tristan's jaw sagged open while Daniel's brows shot up.

"B-Beloveds?" Tristan stuttered. "Both of them?"

Daniel waved his hand and shook his head. "Uh, not to be rude, but Aiden's been around for years, and you never claimed him as your beloved before." Then his eyes narrowed, and he stared at Pestilence. "And no offense, but what kind of name is Pestilence?"

Pestilence smirked as he leaned forward, also keeping his voice low. "I am Pestilence, one of the Four Horsemen of the Apocalypse." He winked. "*That* Pestilence." Resting his hand on the back of Aiden's chair, he smiled as he glanced between the pair. "And we are bonded through my blood, so we are his beloveds."

"Holy shit," Tristan whispered.

Daniel opened his mouth, but Garrett lifted a hand, stalling him as the waitress approached.

"Here we are, gentlemen." Diana placed their drinks on the table, smiling at the group. "Your appetizers should be out in just a couple of minutes. Are you ready to order?"

Aiden smiled sweetly and told her, "Sorry. We were catching up." Lifting the menu, he added, "We haven't even looked, yet."

Nodding, Diana told them, "I'll check up on you in a few."

After Diana had left, Garrett leaned forward again. The other vampires did the same, and he began to explain from the beginning. When he reached the part where he'd been knocked unconscious, Pestilence cut in.

Pestilence explained about his meeting with Master Condor and his subsequent swiping Garrett from the estate.

They paused once when Diana brought their appetizers. After a quick glance at the menu, they all ordered a variation of the burger and fries. Daniel asked for onion rings instead.

By the time their meals arrived, Daniel and Tristan were glancing around in obvious shock.

Finally, Daniel picked up an onion ring. He squished it, then fit the end into a pale red sauce. After soaking it, he popped the fried food into his mouth.

Pestilence eyed his burger. Due to Aiden's urging, he'd added bacon and cheese. Picking it up, he lifted it to his lips and took a big bite. Flavors burst across his tongue, drawing a surprised moan of pleasure from him. Pestilence chewed appreciatively.

Aiden grinned at him as Pestilence swallowed and took another bite.

"Not your usual fair?" Tristan smiled, mirth filling his dark eyes. "Or don't you need to eat at all?"

"Not my usual fair," Pestilence admitted after swallowing. Staring at his fries, he set down his burger. So far, all the stuff he'd tried had tasted delicious. Following Aiden's guidance, Pestilence dipped the end of the fry into a dollop of ketchup before popping it into his mouth. Humming appreciatively, he chewed and swallowed before saying, "That's delicious, too."

Daniel winked at him, then turned to Garrett. "I didn't find your wallet, Gar, but I have the other stuff you asked for." He picked up the second half of his burger. Before taking a bite, Daniel nudged Tristan. "Guess we're gonna be looking for a new coven, huh?"

Tristan nodded as he swallowed his own bite of burger. "Yep." Then he frowned as he glanced around the group. "Although, now that I come to think of it, when was the last time one of our members transferred out?"

"Huh." Garrett cocked his head. "Damn. Before Condor took over."

Daniel made a sound of agreement.

"Is that not normal for a coven?" Pestilence asked curiously.

"Normally, we—" Tristan paused and smiled as Diana approached.

"Anyone need a refill?" Diana asked, glancing at their empty glasses and mugs. "Dessert?"

"I'll take another *Druid Fluid* and a piece of your peach cobbler, please," Aiden told her.

Everyone ordered a refill, and the vampires asked for a second of each appetizer as well as a chili-cheese fry.

Diana's eyes widened, but she didn't question them.

Pestilence eased back in his chair and slung his arm along the back of Aiden's. Full and comfortable, he listened to the vampires whisper about the oddness of their coven letting new members in but none were leaving. He learned that under normal circumstances, if a vampire wasn't part of the inner circle, they transferred out after several decades. Either that or they stayed on the coven grounds and used donors.

Garrett and his buddies had all transferred in at the same time, so for them to ask to move on wouldn't seem suspicious. His friends planned to put in the transfer request and keep Garrett posted. Daniel handed over something he referred to as a burner phone.

His vampire nodded, so he seemed to understand.

Clearing his throat, Pestilence reminded, "That kind of technology doesn't work in"—he paused and glanced around—"where we live."

"Is there any way for them to contact me there?" Garrett asked as he grabbed the last potato skin and dipped it in a tub of ranch dressing.

"There is," Pestilence confirmed, turning his attention to Daniel and Tristan. He pinned them both with a hard stare. "But you can never share it with anyone. Not even your master."

Daniel and Tristan exchanged a look, then nodded.

"Especially not him," Tristan muttered. He tossed his napkin on his empty plate. "Can't believe the shit he tried to pull, but I know you're not lying about it."

Pestilence finished his second glass of wine, then rose to his feet. "We should finish this conversation in the park." He met Garrett's gaze.

What I must do cannot be done here.

Garrett nodded and rose. Then he paused. "Uh, can you get the tab, Daniel?" He grimaced, reminding, "No wallet. Remember?"

"I can pay," Aiden offered, climbing to his feet. "I got mine from the hospital."

"Naw, don't worry about it," Daniel countered, pulling out his wallet. "I got this. Just let me find the waitress."

While Daniel took care of the check, the rest trooped out of the restaurant.

"Oh shit," Tristan muttered, then began herding them to the left. "Around the corner. Now."

"What's wrong?" Pestilence asked, although he allowed the clearly upset vampire to guide him around the corner.

"I just spotted Colby," Tristan told them. "I don't want him to see you."

Pestilence glanced over his shoulder, but he didn't know who he was supposed to be looking for. "Why not just alter his memory?"

Garrett groaned and not in a good way. "He's one of the small population that are immune."

"Ah." Pestilence chuckled. "I would not have that problem."

Aiden snickered. "Right. Forgot about that."

Just as Pestilence started to grin, he felt the snap of a bond reverberate through his mind. He stopped and gasped. Sadness at the loss flooded him.

"Hey, you okay?" Aiden slipped his hand into Pestilence's and squeezed. "You're hurting. What's wrong?"

Pestilence felt Garrett's arm around his waist from the other side. "Pestilence?" his vampire questioned. "What's up?"

"I just lost another—" Pestilence just caught himself from saying the word demon right there on the street. He shook his head. "I've never lost so many in succession unless in battle."

"Okay, time to hurry, then," Garrett stated. "Let's get to the park." He told Tristan which park. "Meet us there. We'll get our stuff, you'll get a contact device, and then we can get home. Okay?"

Sighing, Pestilence nodded.

"I'll be right behind you," Tristan promised. "Here comes Daniel now."

Pestilence wrapped his arms around his men and guided them into the alley. Once hidden from view, he zipped them along a lei line. He reappeared in the park.

Plucking a different strand, Pestilence called to the demon general he knew was on duty in his realm. His bonded minions rotated duties, so they could spend most of their time with their *aminas*—their souls. Maiersto was the demon currently residing in the demon realm.

By the time Maiersto showed up, Garrett's friends had arrived.

Pestilence ordered Maiersto to check on his newly deceased minion's task and to be careful. Considering the dead demon had been over five hundred years old and quite savvy, his death raised Pestilence's suspicion . . . especially since his demon had been right there in Philadelphia . . . again.

What the hell is going on?

CHAPTER ELEVEN

Aiden ached for Pestilence. He didn't know how it had happened, but over the course of ten days, he'd managed to fall in love with the horseman. Seeing Garrett's frown of frustration, plus the pain in his eyes, told Aiden his amazing vampire was in the same boat.

"I have an idea, and I don't like it," Garrett muttered, grimacing. He wrapped his arms around Aiden and pulled him close, tucking his head against his neck. "I think it's my old coven."

Gasping, Aiden murmured, "Would Second Dale really endorse the random murders of demons?" Then he groaned. "Ugh! Not like he'd be able to go against his master without taking over the coven."

"Right," Garrett growled under his breath. "I need to call Daniel."

"You really think Daniel would know?" Aiden nuzzled his lips against Garrett's temple. "And that third demon died just this morning. No way is Pestilence going to agree to take us to the human realm."

Just saying those words still boggled Aiden's mind. He'd nearly died, been saved by a Horseman of the Apocalypse, and now lived with him in the demon realm. That realm happened to be broken into four sections, each ruled by one of the brothers.

"All I have to do is pop in, make the call, and pop back out again," Garrett told him. "I'm going to ask General Abyzou."

Aiden's eyes lit up. "Of course!"

General Abyzou had bonded with a vampire — Toni — that was part of a coven located in Arizona. Toni was part of the inner circle, and they stayed there much of the time. The general happened to be on duty that week.

"Abyzou can take you to an area around that other coven. Not even in the same state, so you'll be safe." Another thought struck Aiden, and he grimaced. "But Pestilence will be pissed when you get back."

Garrett shook his head. "I'll tell him," he assured. "I'm just not going to take no for an answer."

"Do you, um, do you want me to come?" Aiden didn't really want to go, but he had to offer.

Chuckling, Garrett used his arm around Aiden to begin leading him out of their suite. "Uh, no offense, sweetheart." He winked. "You still pass out when you travel through the mists. This is going to be quick, so you wouldn't even remember anything."

Aiden nodded. That made sense. "Promise to stay safe."

Garrett dipped his head and kissed his cheek. "Always."

Ten minutes later, Pestilence glared at Garrett. "If that is the case, then allow me to ask them directly," their horseman demanded, thrusting his finger through his hair. "It would be far simpler."

Sighing, Garrett rubbed his palms over Pestilence's pectorals. "And then you would level the coven for the sins of a few." Sliding his hands up to cradle Pestilence's cheeks, he stated, "Let me find out for sure. Then we'll deal with it."

"We?" Pestilence narrowed his eyes even as he allowed Garrett to press their foreheads together. "What do you mean by that?"

"I mean, his behavior constitutes an act of war against another paranormal body." Garrett hardened his voice. "The

Vampire Council frowns on that sort of thing without permission."

Growling under his breath, Pestilence slid his hands up and down Garrett's neck, finally settling on his shoulders. "I should be the one to take you."

"You're busy shuffling demons," Garrett countered. "I'll ask General Abyzou to take me to a safe place, and I'll get ahold of either Daniel or Tristan."

"Gods," Pestilence grumbled. "I hate it when you're all logical. I need to find a demon to replace this morning's fallen, and the fates suddenly decided to spread a plague across southern Africa."

Garrett pecked a kiss to Pestilence's lips, then eased away. "Let me do this for you, my chosen horseman." He tugged on Pestilence's hair. "I'll be back before you can miss me."

"Not true," Pestilence muttered. "I miss you every damn time you're not within touching distance." He glanced Aiden's way. "You and Aiden both."

Chuckling, Garrett whispered, "We love you, too."

Pestilence jerked his head up, his eyes rounding. "What?"

Smiling, Aiden closed the last few steps between them. He'd been giving Garrett a chance to tell their lover his plan without his involvement.

Not anymore, though.

"We do love you, Pestilence." Aiden wrapped his right arm around his horseman's waist and placed his other on his chest. He traced his palm over Pestilence's slender, defined torso. "Guess we all need to learn to express ourselves better, huh?"

Garrett chuckled. "Yeah." Then he pecked Aiden's lips and backed up a step.

"Wait," Pestilence growled, his eyes narrowing. His body practically vibrated under Aiden's touch, so he squeezed tightly and flicked his fingertip over Pestilence's nipple through his tunic. His lover growled and focused on him.

"Stop trying to distract me with sex."

Aiden felt his face heat, and he ducked his head.

Pestilence cupped his jaw, urging him to tilt his face up. "Not that I don't love it." He pecked a slow sipping kiss to Aiden's lips, licking and nuzzling. "But this is too important."

"What is it?" Garrett asked, cocking his head.

"I love you both, too," Pestilence stated, glancing between them. "If anything were to happen to either of you, I would cast a pox on whoever hurt you and everyone they knew."

Aiden's heart skipped a beat. "Damn," he whispered. Unable to help himself, he grinned. "That mental image should *not* make my cock throb, but it does."

Garrett laughed, bumping his shoulder into Aiden's. "It's a paranormal thing." Then he cradled Pestilence's jaw and kissed him lightly before pulling away. "I'll be back before you know it."

"Going somewhere?"

Turning his head, Aiden spotted Abyzou lounging in the doorway. He figured Pestilence had done that weird summoning trick. The winged demon smiled at him, his silver-gray eyes dancing with mirth.

Pestilence nodded as he drew away from Garrett. "You will take my chosen vampire to a safe place, provide him with a phone, and watch over him as he makes a phone call or two." He returned his attention to Garrett. "You be careful."

"Always," Garrett replied, touching Pestilence's lips with his fingertips. "See you soon."

Abyzou bowed slightly. "I'll care for him as my own."

Then they were gone.

Aiden sighed. "As much as I want to help you figure out what's going on with your demons" — he tipped his head up to meet Pestilence's gaze — "I don't want to think that the people I lived with for the last few years could do this."

"I understand that feeling," Pestilence told him, pecking a

kiss to his lips. "And as much as I wish I could spend the hours while he's gone fucking, so time will fly" — he waggled his brows — "I do have to get this illness started."

Nodding, Aiden eased away from Pestilence. "I really do understand." He made a shooing motion with his hands as he winked. "Just don't think you're taking your horse."

Pestilence laughed as he grinned. "Noted. I'll have to go on foot."

Giggling, Aiden turned and bounced out of the room. He changed into a pair of riding breeches and a comfortable tunic similar in cut to Pestilence's. Then he went in search of his horseman's mount.

Over the last couple of days, Aiden had discovered he loved horseback riding, and Pestilence's mare took ever-so-good care of him.

"You must be one of Pestilence's men."

Hearing the deep voice behind him, Aiden nearly toppled off the horse. He grabbed the pommel just in time, keeping him upright. Turning, he gasped.

Holy shit! Pestilence!

Aiden couldn't help himself. Never again would he allow himself to freeze. That didn't mean he could stop the dark spots that threatened to obscure his breathing quite so easily.

Gripping his saddle, Aiden struggled to control his breathing as a tremble worked through his body.

Aiden? What's wrong?

Pestilence's voice sounded through his mind, but Aiden couldn't make himself focus enough to respond. To his shame, a whimper escaped his throat.

"Hey? You okay, human?" the hulking, black-skinned male asked, sounding confused . . . and maybe even a little concerned. "It's Aiden, right?"

Even as Aiden nodded, a little brown head popped up from a saddlebag on the mount of the paranormal who could only be War. The creature appeared to be some kind of rodent. It chittered, sounding upset.

War frowned as he glanced between them. "I didn't mean to, Xerxes. He's riding Pestilence's horse." Rolling his eyes at whatever the animal's response was, he grumbled, "I thought he would know who I am. Not like I'm going to harm my brother's chosen." After a huffing sigh, War muttered, "Fine."

Then War maneuvered his massive black horse closer. Pestilence's mare didn't react, indicating that they must know each other. In the next instant, the rodent hopped out of War's saddlebag and settled on his horse's pommel.

Chittering softly, the animal rested its front claws on Aiden's chest. It stretched up and vocalized quietly. At the same time, it managed to pet his cheek . . . and it didn't even scratch him.

"Aww, you're okay, little buddy," War rumbled. "Do me a favor and tell Xerxes that you're okay." He grimaced. "I don't wanna be sleepin' on the couch tonight."

Aiden, answer me!

Between the animal petting him, War's comments, and Pestilence's calls, Aiden managed to calm down enough to focus. He answered his lover first.

I'm okay. Just a sec.

Then Aiden focused on the animal—Xerxes. Remembering that was the name of War's shifter chosen, he understood the huge black-skinned horseman's comments better. He glanced between them, then forced a smile as he looked at Xerxes.

"I'm okay. Really. Just—" Aiden paused and nibbled his lip for a second. He felt his face heat as embarrassment flooded him. Focusing on War, Aiden admitted, "You startled me, and I had a bad run-in not too long ago with a vampire. I know you're not a vampire, but you're clearly paranormal, and Pestilence never showed me a picture of any of his brothers, and I—" Aiden snapped his mouth shut and mentally groaned. Finally, he managed to whisper, "Sorry."

Xerxes chittered once more, and Aiden smiled at the shifter. "I'm okay. Really." He tapped his temple. "Just still sorting stuff in my head."

Nodding, Xerxes chirped once more, then jumped back into War's saddlebag.

Aiden? What's going on, my sweet?

Your brother showed up. Um, War. He, uh . . . he sort of startled me. I freaked a little. I didn't mean to, um . . .

Say no more. Pestilence sounded kind, even in Aiden's mind. *Tell him I'll be there soon. I'm almost done here.*

Will do. Aiden glanced at a waiting, and amused looking, War. *Should I offer him refreshments or something?*

Pestilence chuckled through their connection.

Sure. Take him to the office. There's finger foods and mead in the refrigerator. Don't feel like you have to entertain him, my chosen.

Pleased to have something to do, Aiden nodded absently. Then he realized his lover couldn't see him. *Okay. Love you.*

A surge of affection filtered through their connection.

Love you, too, Aiden.

Clearing his throat, Aiden couldn't stop his grin as he focused on War. "So, um, yeah. This way." He turned Pestilence's mount and started toward the front of the estate. Realizing who he was talking to, he snorted. "I guess you know the way, huh?"

"Still nice to be invited," War told him. "Where's Pestilence? I assume you were just communicating with him."

Aiden nodded. "He's on an errand. He should be back shortly." Then he scowled at War. "You're not here to decapitate him again, are you?"

War tipped his horned head back and great booming laughter erupted from him.

That gave Aiden a few seconds to take in the horseman's massive, black-skinned and heavily muscled frame. He had large red horns that curved back from his head. His eyes were red as were his huge, bat-like wings.

Aiden had only seen Pestilence's wings twice. They weren't quite as large, and they were a stormy-gray color. His lover didn't normally keep them out. Aiden's fingers twitched thinking about them, and he wondered if he could convince his horseman to change that.

"He told you about that, huh?" War asked, still sporting a grin.

"Just that it happened during a war," Aiden admitted.

War continued to grin. "Well, there's far more to that story. Maybe I'll tell you while we wait for Pestilence to get back."

Aiden didn't know if he wanted to hear War's version of events. Unfortunately, he didn't know how he could get out of it, either.

Chapter Twelve

Garrett strode into Pestilence's study, General Abyzou flanking him. Spotting the massive, red-winged male taking up nearly the entire leather love seat — as well as the small, sweat-pants-clad man on his lap — he froze. Relief filled Garrett when he spotted Aiden pouring drinks into tumblers at the sidebar.

"Hey, sweetheart," Garrett greeted, announcing his presence before his lover could pick up the drink's platter. "Everything okay?"

Aiden spun and grinned. "Hey, you're back," he cried. Leaving the bar, he hustled toward him. "Are you well?"

Wrapping Aiden in his arms, Garrett dipped his head and pressed a hard kiss to his lips. "I am." Then he straightened and peered at the amused expression on the horned man's lips as well as the beaming smile on the little man's. "Uh, is everything okay here? Where's Pestilence?"

"He's just finishing up an errand," Aiden told him. Then he swung his hand and indicated the strangers. "This is War and War's shifter chosen, Xerxes. Everyone" — Aiden indicated him — "this is Garrett."

"Hi," Xerxes called, waving and grinning. "Nice to meet you."

"And you," Garrett responded instinctively. Then he dipped his chin in greeting to the massive horseman. "War."

Appearing amused, War winked. "Garrett."

Aiden squeezing his wrist drew Garrett's attention. "Is it what you thought?"

90

Garrett grimaced. "Yeah."

Sighing, Aiden stared at the floor. His expression turned crest-fallen. "Damn."

"Aiden? Garrett?" Pestilence swept into the room and instantly pulled them both to his chest. "Gods, I've been worried." After planting a deep kiss on each of their lips, he nodded at his brother. "War. Xerxes. Welcome."

War rose. "Thanks, brother." Instead of crossing to Pestilence, however, he headed to the sideboard and the forgotten drinks. Picking up one, he tossed back the contents. "So." He refilled his drink, picked up a second from the tray, and returned to Xerxes. "Do you mind telling me who you pissed off in Philadelphia?"

"Ah, fuck." Garrett groaned. "Are they killing your demons, too?"

Arching a brow, War handed a drink to Xerxes. "I've lost two in that area in the last week and a half," he told them before taking a sip.

"Fuck," Garrett repeated, scrubbing his palm over his face. Turning his focus to Pestilence, he nodded. "It's Condor, Rizer, and Whitney, as far as I can tell from my call with Daniel."

Using his hold around both their waists, Pestilence guided them forward. "Please explain. As far as you can tell?"

Garrett nodded, following Pestilence's urging. "Tristan left the line open when he tracked down Second Dale," he told everyone. Seeing War's arched brow, he added, "He's one of my best friends from my old coven. Someone I trust with my life." Waving his hand, Garrett got back on track. "Anyway, Tristan tracked down the second and bluntly stated that he'd heard our coven had started demon hunting, and he asked if it was true." Garrett winced, saying, "Second Dale heaved a sigh and admitted to seeing Master Condor, Enforcer Rizer, and Enforcer Whitney heading out after the master took a private phone call. The second didn't know who the call was from, however."

"Soooo . . ." War's eyes narrowed. "Someone is tracking the comings and goings of demons and . . . is Master Condor an ex-master? You didn't leave on good terms?"

Pestilence shook his head. "He beat Garrett and refused to honor my bond. I removed him from the coven."

War heaved a sigh. "So he's taking it out on any demon he can track down in his city. Great." After knocking back his glass, he rose to his feet. "Come on. I happen to know Death has lost a demon, too, but I don't know about Famine."

"He's not normally in that area," Pestilence commented, and War nodded.

Xerxes quickly rose, setting aside his barely sipped drink. War took his hand and guided him to the door. "Let's go, guys. Time to decide if playing by the rules is necessary or if we can take matters into our own hands."

Pestilence urged Garrett and Aiden after his brother. "What did you have in mind?"

When War smiled over his shoulder at Pestilence, his expression appeared a little feral. "My other chosen, Monte, is working with his coven, at the moment. We'll visit them and ask." Then War smirked. "And I'm contacting Death to join us, since we know the bastards have impacted him, too. I'll send one of my generals to inquire with Famine."

Garrett remembered Pestilence telling him about his brothers and their beloveds. Monte was the head enforcer for a coven out in Montana. He still worked closely with his fellow vampires because they'd accepted his bonding with War.

Smart move.

Less than ten minutes later, Garrett looked over the sprawling ranch before him. He spotted a half dozen people standing on the porch, mostly wearing flannels, boots, and jeans.

The woman sported a peasant skirt and blouse and stood in the embrace of a broad-shouldered vampire.

A redhead dropped off the porch and swiftly strode toward them. War opened his arms and accepted the man's embrace, which Xerxes was included in. The vampire sank into a deep kiss with War, which lasted more than was appropriate. Once they broke apart, the vampire kissed Xerxes, too.

That has to be Monte.

As they finished up, movement to Garrett's left caught his attention. He spotted Death approaching. With him were two humans, a wide-shouldered dark-haired man as well as a slenderer blond.

Daren and Eric.

Although Garrett wasn't certain which was which.

"Give it a rest," Death called, amusement lacing his words. "You said you had news?" Turning to Garrett, Death smiled. "You look a sight better." Then he dipped his chin at Aiden. "And you must be Aiden. Nice to officially meet you. I'm Death." He pointed at the dark-haired man, then the blond. "My chosens, Daren and Eric."

After that, introductions to those on the deck were quickly made. Coven Master Dante Mannis was the one holding the skirt-clad, Ruth. The dark-haired vampire was Second Kellan Harlon. The massive, black-skinned male was actually one of War's demons—Thanach, and he held his blond human *amina*, Giles Corsair.

"So, War," Dante began once everyone was seated on the massive back deck. "Monte said you had something odd come up that I may be able to help with?" He peered around at War's brothers, interest filling his hazel eyes. "Something affecting all of you?"

Ruth and the human donor, Hank, hurried around getting everyone drinks.

War didn't sugar coat it.

"If you decided to start picking off demons willy-nilly because you were pissed that I bonded with a vampire from your coven, could I take out your inner circle?"

Master Dante's brows shot up, and everyone stared in surprise.

Shrugging, War continued, "Or is there some vampire enforcers I could contact to make you stop?"

"W-Well," Master Dante stuttered, expressing his shock just as surely as his scent did. He cleared his throat, then nodded. "Yes, you could contact the Vampire Council. They would assign a diplomat and a couple of council enforcers to act as liaisons while you met with the coven master to air your grievances."

Huffing a sigh, War crossed his arms over his chest. "I'd much rather just kill the bastards."

"Me, too," Pestilence grumbled.

Garrett took his hand and squeezed it. "I'm sorry my coven master is causing everyone such problems."

Pestilence scoffed. "Your asshole *ex*-coven leader is to blame," he stated coldly, pinning him with a narrow-eyed expression. "Not you. All you wanted to do was accept my bond to save someone you love." Pestilence lifted Aiden with one arm from his nearby deck chair and placed him on his lap. Aiden immediately relaxed against him. "Someone we both now love. We'll make those fuckers pay."

War growled, then nodded. "Master Dante, could you please contact whoever you need to? The master of the Philadelphia Rutherford coven is attacking our demons." Then he narrowed his eyes. "And the only way he'd know when they showed up in his city is with magick."

"Uh, I didn't know anyone in my coven—"

"*Ex*-coven," Pestilence again corrected.

"*Ex*-coven had contact with magick," Garrett finished.

War grinned broadly, the expression malicious. "We'll be

sure to find a chance to ask your ex-master about that."

Dante pulled his cell phone from his belt and dialed a number. "I'd like to report an infraction perpetrated by a coven master brought to me by another paranormal group."

Whoever Dante was talking to made things move pretty swiftly after that.

Garrett sat in the back of a large, *Hummer*-style limousine with nearly a dozen others. As much as he wished he could leave Aiden behind for the confrontation, he knew his lover wouldn't have heard of it. Pestilence sat on their human's other side.

Pestilence's three brothers had joined them. While Famine hadn't personally had any demons killed, that was only because none of his minions had worked in the area recently. If they had, they would have been targeted.

The rest in the limo were there representing the Vampire Council. There were two diplomats—Caspian Carpathian and Sebastian Russo. The two enforcers were Vincent Marché and Nereo Belmonte. The final man in the vehicle was Vince's wolf shifter beloved, Frankie Drunger. He remained quiet and watchful, obviously there to watch his mate's back.

As soon as the vehicle pulled up to the gate, it opened. *Nice.*

As the home Garrett had shared with many others over the last several decades came into view, unease twisted in his gut.

Aiden squeezed his thigh. "Relax," he whispered. "We'll be safe."

"I didn't want you to come. I don't want you in the line of fire," Garrett reminded him.

Smiling lovingly at him, Aiden stated, "I know. But I'll be fine." He reached his other hand for Pestilence. "I have you guys. I don't need anything else, and nothing anyone says can change that."

"Damn straight," Pestilence growled.

Garrett sighed and nodded. "What he said."

The limo stopped under the portico, and whoever sat next to the driver up front climbed out. He spoke briefly with someone, then opened the back door. Instead of backing away to let them out, he stuck his head in the door.

"Fair warning," he muttered softly. "They're claiming a countersuit that Pestilence kidnapped one of their vampires, and they only killed demons to get his attention so he'd return him."

Sebastian smirked. "Ah, so they know why we're here." He winked at Pestilence. "We'll get this cleared up quickly enough."

Growling softly, Pestilence snarled, "Kidnapped? I rescued him from a locked cell where he'd been left beaten and bloody." He curled his lip as grumbles went through the other horsemen. "He's lucky I didn't just pop in and slay the entire inner circle for his crimes against my chosen."

Lifting his hands in placation, Caspian murmured soothing words. "We do appreciate that. Very much," he assured. "Now, let us do our jobs and take out the trash, leaving the good ones behind. Okay?"

Pestilence snarled once more, then cleared his features. "Let's do this."

War smirked. Death chuckled. Even a glimmer of amusement appeared in Famine's pale eyes.

Everyone exited the limo.

Garrett spotted the inner circle and extra guards lined up along the steps leading to the house.

So they don't even plan to let us in. Not good to insult council representatives that way.

"Coven Master Condor," Sebastian began, locking his gaze on the vampire. "Perhaps it would be best to step inside to a more private setting?"

While it was spoken as a question, Garrett knew it wasn't.

Master Condor shook his head once as he crossed his arms

over his chest. "I don't think so, Representative Russo." He narrowed his eyes as he focused on the horsemen. "I've had kidnappers in my house before and won't have it again."

Yep. An idiot.

"Thank you for returning my coven-member to me," Condor continued. Snapping his fingers, he pointed at his feet. "Come, Garrett. You're safe to leave them now."

Not just an idiot.

Unable to help himself, Garrett laughed. He wrapped his arms around his waist, doubling over. Tears leaked from the corners of his eyes as he shook, leaning into Aiden to stay upright.

"What the fuck?" Enforcer Rizer snarled.

"Shut it," Enforcer Caine snapped, glaring at the lower level enforcer. When Rizer opened his mouth again, obviously intending to mouth off, Caine pointed his thick finger at him. "Don't make me repeat myself."

Garrett figured Caine had no idea that Rizer had ended up one of Condor's favorites.

"Leave him be, Caine," Condor ordered. "Or you'll lose your position."

Caine clenched his jaw and fell silent. Rizer smirked snidely. Second Dale's eyes narrowed, and he glanced around surreptitiously. Surprisingly, Maude nodded almost imperceptibly.

"If you return my people," Condor began again. "I'll stop killing your demons."

"People is it now?" Caspian commented drolly. "Before it was just Garrett. Who is the *people* now?"

Condor's face flushed a smidge, but he pointed at Aiden. "Our donor, Aiden Rolston." His eyes narrowed. "We must deal with him our way, too."

"Your way?" Famine hissed, clearly annoyed by the man. "What is *your* way?" The man clutched a sheath of wheat in his hand, and it twitched, showing his agitation.

Garrett suddenly realized that War wasn't the hothead of the group. That title clearly belonged to Famine. The horseman practically itched to attack those who'd harmed his brothers' minions.

Glaring at Famine, Condor sneered at him. "How I care for those in my coven is my business."

"Actually, it's *our* business," Sebastian stated. "A coven master has no authority to deny his members requests to transfer, especially after being in the area for over four decades." He pulled out some paperwork. "Daniel and Tristan, the Vampire Council overrides Master Condor's refusal and approves your request to switch covens."

"You can't do that," Condor roared, jumping forward a step. "Those are *my* people, and they'll do as I say."

"I challenge you for the right of the coven," Dale bellowed, turning to face Condor. "Face me."

"What?" Clearly shocked, Condor gaped at Dale. "How could you?"

"You're no longer putting the safety of our coven first," Dale told him, his features dark with anger. His hazel eyes glimmered in the evening light. "You're putting your own selfish desires to control and manipulate above our peoples' safety. It's time you step down."

"Never!" Condor yelled. "Seize him."

While Rizer and Whitney instantly moved to obey, Caine and Maude easily yanked them back and subdued them.

Dale lunged forward and swept out a leg. Condor went down. Glaring at the clearly shocked now-*ex*-coven master, Dale ordered, "I want you packed and in that limo with the council enforcers when they leave, Condor. You, Rizer, and Whitney are no longer welcome here." Without removing his gaze from Condor, Dale raised his voice and called, "Can he go with you, Enforcers?"

"Of course," Victor immediately replied. "They're being

charged with the murder of a number of demons." The council enforcer chuckled coldly. "They would have been coming with us anyway."

"And we'll report the status changes to this coven," Caspian stated, as if what had happened was the most normal thing in the world.

Condor curled his lip. "You won't get away with this."

Dale arched one brow and waved his hand to indicate those around him. "I'm being supported by council representatives, enforcers in the coven, and the Four fucking Horsemen of the Apocalypse." He scoffed. "All because you couldn't let one vampire and his favorite blood donor go. Did you invite that rogue into our area, too?" Then the blood drained from Dale's face, and his eyes widened. "Holy fuck! You did! You tried to have Aiden killed because he would only sleep with Garrett."

"You bastard," Garrett screamed, lunging forward.

Pestilence's deceptively strong arms wrapped around his waist and hauled him back. "Relax," his horseman purred into his ear. "He's not worth it. He's done."

Garrett groaned and shuddered, even as he nodded. He gripped Pestilence's wrist while grabbing Aiden with his free arm. He hauled his human against him.

It took Garrett a few seconds to realize Aiden whispered, "It's okay. I'm safe. You and Pestilence saved me."

Finally, Garrett managed to take a deep enough breath to clear his head. He nodded. Then he pressed a kiss to Aiden's temple. When he lifted his head, he couldn't seem to find words.

"Well, damn," War rumbled, grinning. "That was fun." He patted Pestilence on the back, then winked at Garrett and Aiden. "Don't be a stranger now." Turning away, between one step and the next, War disappeared. Somehow, his words lingered in the air. "Toppling an asshole vampire leader without a war. Huh."

Death chuckled and shook his head. "See you later, guys. I'll bring my men by to meet you properly before too long." Then, he was gone, too.

Garrett took in Famine's cold, pleased smile as he watched a bunch of vampires drag a sullen Rizer, a screaming Condor, and a confused Whitney into the house.

He assumed it was to pack a few things.

Famine hummed as he turned his pale-blue-eyed gaze on Pestilence. "I see why you all have started paying more attention to the human realm." Grinning, he glanced behind him at Dale. His look could only be called heated. "There are those here that are . . . interesting."

A second later, Famine disappeared.

Blowing out a breath, Garrett realized they were the only ones left standing under the portico. He shook his head and focused on his men. "Time to take us home, Pestilence."

"Home?" His horseman sounded uncertain.

Grinning, Garrett nodded. "Yep. *Home*, so I can fuck you both through the mattress."

Aiden snickered. "Oh, yeah. *Home*."

Pestilence growled and wrapped his arms around them both. "*Home*."

In the next instant, they were the ones to disappear . . . and Garrett could hardly wait for them to reappear.

Home.

ABOUT THE AUTHOR

Charlie started writing fantasy when she was eight, and after stumbling onto her first erotic romance at age nineteen, she realized her true calling. She now focuses on writing gay erotic romance, normally of the paranormal variety, with heroes of all kinds. With the help and support of her husband, Charlie finally fulfilled one of her life-long goals . . . move to acreage with her horses. You can often find her curled up with her laptop and a cup of tea or glass of wine, creating her next adventure. Charlie enjoys exploring the mountains of her new Oregon home on horseback, 4-wheeler, or motorcycle.

She can be reached at ch.richards2010@yahoo.com

Or visit her at www.charlie-richards.com